BRENDAN MALONE: THE LAST FENIAN

MARINA J. NEARY

ALL THINGS THAT MATTER PRESS

ISBN: 978-0-9846297-4-9

Library of Congress Control Number: 2010919433

Author Photo by Richard Megenis
Cover Design by All Things that Matter Press
Cover photo by Walter Lawrence Neary
Published in 2011 by All Things that Matter Press

For hundreds of years the British tried to conquer Ireland and the Irish fought back. From that struggle great legends appeared: tales of heroes and traitors, of love and suffering, and always, always of the human spirit. With *Brendan Malone* M.J. Neary has added a well-crafted and finely researched novel to the genre.

--Kenneth Weene, author: *Widow's Walk* and *Memoirs From the Asylum*

The author has brought a difficult period of Irish history to life through a combination of historical and fictional characters. The effect of this tragic period on an Irish family is heartbreaking. The characters are well developed and very easy to make a personal connection with. This is a tragic tale of how blind devotion to a cause can wreak utter destruction and cause you to lose all that you love.

--Jim Dougherty, President of *The Wild Geese*

With unerring precision the multitalented Neary meticulously unfolds a family drama within the framework of the much bigger Irish drama that took place in the beginning of the 20th century. The showdown between father and son in this tale is the equivalent of a downright show stopper. The romance of the younger brother has the beauty of a Jane Austen tale. But at the end it all amounts to an Irish tragedy.

--Bertil Falk, translator of *Locked Rooms and Open Spaces*

Brendan Malone is a tragedy set in Ireland during the decade preceding the Easter Rebellion of 1916. With a discerning understanding of the political and socio-economic conflicts of the period, Neary skillfully weaves a dramatic narrative of a house divided, love and hatred, betrayal and revenge, guilt and expiation. Intellectually engaging, intense and visceral, *Brendan Malone* is a gripping read from beginning to end.

> --Gary Inbinder, author of *Confessions of the Creature*

Neary's skill and artistry with deftly handling the Irish dialect are on full display here. Lush and delicious. Constantly surprising, thoroughly entertaining.

> --Joel Vetsch, director of "C.S. Bukowski", named top film, by *The Guardian*

Neary grabs you with her first sentence, holds you by the lapels, and doesn't release you till she's finished with you, as is her want. This time around, it's the tragedy of a delusional father dragging his sons to their deaths. Meticulously researched, the novel provides a behind-the-scenes glimpse into the lesser known aspects of the Irish history.

> --Julian Padowicz, author of *Writer's Block*

Marina Neary, who has always been deeply inspired by Gaelic history and Victor Hugo's romanticism, knows how to set stage for a historical tragedy. *Brendan Malone* carries the reader across the wild open space of central Ireland. Tirades on patriotism and treachery blow over the land like haunting gales. The strong characters make the reader feel the violent spirit of independence, the changing skies and the precarious atmosphere engulfing the country.

> --Eric Bertrand, author of *Le Ceilidh*

This work is dedicated to my three father figures Julian P., John B. and Walt N., who had so many valid reasons and golden opportunities to strangle me over the years yet have resisted stoically. It takes three men to keep a girl like me in line. Thank you for pointing out my proper place – on the barricades.

Acknowledgments

I would like to thank Kenneth Weene, author of *Widow's Walk* and *Memoirs from the Asylum,* for his invaluable literary and historical guidance that helped me take the manuscript to another level, and Marnie Hay, whose biography *Bulmer Hobson and the Nationalist Movement in Twentieth-Century Ireland* provided me with additional insights into the private lives of various IRB members. Special thanks to the cover models and their families. From left to right: Benjamin Freedman, Joel Vetsch and Alexander Mair. Above all, I would like to thank my fearless and vehemently unorthodox father, Julian P. who taught me to live without fear of being judged.

I started writing *Brendan Malone* in late 1990s, at the height of Celtic Renaissance. At the time I was a freshman in college, working as a research assistant to an Irish history professor who specialized in the early 20th century nationalism. Over the course of our long sessions at the library he had casually imparted a few real life stories from the early 1900s, which, quite honestly, chilled my blood, even though the concept of nationalism was not exactly entirely foreign to me. My own father had experimented with ethnic activism. His endeavors did not go beyond signing petitions and attending meetings, but I know how a seemingly peaceful cultural movement can take an abrupt militant turn in a blink of an eye. The whole issue of national identity is highly volatile.

Little by little, in the winter of 1997 I began creating a story, a folkloric family tragicomedy, leaning primarily on my professor's accounts as well as my own experience. There are characters in Celtic epos whose devotion to their cause often eclipses their natural instincts such as love for their offspring. The act of disowning of one's disobedient child, sometimes to the extreme of filicide, is a common theme in Irish and Scottish myths and folk tales. In the decade preceding the rising of 1916, the state of the Irish Republican Brotherhood (IRB) alternatively known as the Fenian Brotherhood, the most prominent nationalistic organization, was rather disheartening. As Bulmer Hobson and Denis McCullough began reviving the movement in the North of Ireland, pouring young blood and fresh ideas into the dying organization, all sorts of chemical reactions erupted within the Brotherhood. The word "traitor" became a very popular label that was applied quite liberally to anyone who did not follow in the footsteps of the ringleader.

Over the years I have published several essays and articles dealing with Irish history, including one on Hugh O'Neill, the Earl of Tyrone. My readers often ask me: "Whose side are you on? Are you with the Irish rebels or with the British imperialists?" I have successfully eluded giving a straightforward answer. Usually I reply: "It is not one's right to freedom that I question but the methods of obtaining it." It is important to remember that questioning is not the same as condemning. As a historical novelist with considerable personal ties to the subject, I must tread with particular caution, as there is a very fine line about fiction and blatant propaganda. The question of the Irish nationalism will always remain somewhat raw, no matter on which side of the ocean or the political fence you may find yourself. I am neither a moralist nor a politician. My goal as a writer is to leave the reader with more questions than answers. In the words of my father, Julian P., "Beware those who have found the absolute truth, and run from those who are willing to die for it."

PROLOGUE:
The Freak Show On Frankfurt Avenue
(Dublin, 1908)

"Truly, Mama, nothing extraordinary is happening here, just a few tipsy piglets from University College grunting beneath our windows. No, there is no need to splash them with cold water. They are drenched from the rain already. Give my apologies to the guests. I sorely need air."

The stain glass door to the balcony slammed, separating the noise of the festivity inside the villa from the humid March evening.

Left alone, the young girl bent over the carved balustrade and glanced down with a sort of sneering curiosity at the students who appeared more than eager to resume the interrupted conversation with the ravishing brunette.

"Please, explain once again," one of them spoke, struggling to articulate more or less clearly. "The Polish Count isn't your father?"

"Only in spirit, my lamb!" she chirped in response, grasping at the opportunity to talk about her unconventional origin, which, apparently, was as a source of tremendous pride for her. "It is a fact which we both regret at times. Oh, Count Markiewicz is a gallant, humorous, artistic soul. You must see his oil portraits! I am still trying to persuade him to donate a few pieces to the college gallery, but he will not relinquish any. The man's modesty is infuriating! He also writes plays and brings them to stage himself. Otherwise, why would my mother have married him? They met at a ball in Paris ten years ago, long after I was born. I assure you, he loves me no less than he does Stanislas and Maeve, though in blood we aren't related."

The exhausted gramophone behind the curtain of the ballroom began spitting out bits of Oginski's polonaise. The silhouettes, that until then had been wavering chaotically, began forming into a semblance of a line. Count Markiewicz's guests were preparing to celebrate their Slavic glory in the heart of an Irish city.

"If so, then who's your real father?" the student continued interrogating her, which she did not seem to mind at all. "Confess! Who is the lucky bastard who created a beauty like you?"

The girl tossed her head up, as if addressing the moon.

"My father," she droned with almost theatrical pathos, "is a devoted servant of his land —*our* land, that is..."

The student was in no state to solve riddles. For one, he did not know how to interpret the string of the bestial endearments sent in his address. First he was called a piglet, and then promoted to a lamb. What animal would he become by the end of the night? He was secretly hoping to be called a stallion.

"So, is he in that Gaelic League with that fellow by the name Pearse?"

Dropping the names of political activists left and right would surely impress the young lady. The drunken student was incredibly pleased with himself for having even remembered Patrick Pearse. Now the count's stepdaughter would know that he was not merely killing time at University College. No, sir! She was not the only one who appreciated high culture.

"Silly pup!" the girl laughed, causing the student to pull his head into his shoulders. He had been demoted to a pup. "The Gaelic League requires formal education and some serious understanding of poetry, which aren't the strongest merits of my father. Still, he is learned enough for the Republican Brotherhood."

The last two words were delivered in menacing whisper and accompanied by a conspiratorial wink.

The student let his jaw hang, as if someone had punched him in the chest.

"A Fenian...So, you're one of us then!" He shook the empty whiskey bottle over his head triumphantly and then spun around to face his companions. "Hear that? Her father's in the Brotherhood, just like mine."

"And I intend to spend the summer with him," the girl continued proudly. "As soon as I finish paying my duties to the society." She nodded negligently towards the lights and the wavering shadows behind the balcony door. "As soon as I dance the same polonaise ten times over and let every old man pinch my cheek, I'm off to the shores of Shannon, to be with my natural father. Perhaps, I'll meet you there someday."

That was the moment when the student's legs resigned on him. He dropped to his knees, on the pavement, assuming the archetypical Romeo pose, his eyes still fixed on the balcony. At that stage of intoxication he could see only a vague figure in white, all entwined with black hair. His mind proved out to be no less treacherous than his legs, and the student filled the streets with a savage howl, clasping his hands to the chest, just like the early film actors did.

"Blast me! Where the hell are the words when I need 'em? Why can't I be a poet? Wouldn't I cherish you if you were my wife! Let me hang if I lie. Dadaí raised me a patriot. Do you even know my Dadaí? Oh, he's the finest landlord in the whole of Tulsk! He owns two farms, a potato field, and a whole herd of horses like you can't find anywhere else. He also got more rifles and sabers than the whole British army! And all that can be yours, love. Just say a word."

The girl listened to his ranting with an air of superficial fascination. She seemed accustomed to such conduct from men.

Drunken speeches were clearly no novelty to her, even though she was standing on the balcony of the most fashionable villa on Frankfurt Avenue, wearing in a goddess gown of white silk, with golden bracelets of the most meticulous craft clasped around her wrists. She blended quite well into the atmosphere affluence, yet one could sense, there was another place on this earth that would make her an even more welcoming home, another society that would find her qualities even more admirable.

Her behavior was a bit too unbridled for a true aristocrat. She laughed with impermissible sincerity. The clumsy tricks of the drunken student that would have repulsed any young lady only amused the Count's stepdaughter. Irresistible in her jovial audacity, like a heroine from a folk tale, she needed no more than what nature had given her to win instant affections.

Suddenly, the girl bowed even lower over the balustrade, allowing the students to catch a glimpse of what was hidden beneath the shoulder ties of her goddess gown. She held onto the slippery railing with the confidence and the agility of trapeze acrobat, kicking up her feet in golden sandals, her neck arched.

"Wait now, what's your father's name?" she asked squinting quizzically. "Could it be Brendan Malone?"

Once again, the student wavered in awe.

"I'll be damned. How did you know?"

"Oh, it wasn't difficult at all," she replied, straightening out abruptly, thus depriving the smitten boys of the bliss of staring at her bust worthy of Athena. "Who else could have a son so boastful? As it turns out, my dear, our fathers are tight friends. That means I know you, too. And you ought to be ashamed, young Mr. Malone. You have a bride at home, a sweet, trusting, primitive soul. What if she were to see you now and hear your serenades addressed to another woman?"

The student slapped himself on the forehead and let the palm of his hand drag slowly across his flushed face.

"Heavens, that's true, too," he muttered in horror. "I'm drunk, love, deadly drunk. Satan twisted me, I swear."

"Surely, blame it on poor Satan!" The girl frowned skeptically. "And does he twist you often? Do your other lady-friends know about Caitlin?"

"There are no other women, I swear!" he shouted in self-defense. "And I don't drink often. No money, see?" He turned his pockets inside out and let them hanging like a pair of donkey's ears. "Today I spent the last penny of my stipend, but only in the honor of St. Patrick's. That would be a mortal sin not to toast our christener."

"I see now," the count's stepdaughter concluded with a nod. "St. Patrick and Satan are on the same side for once. They united to empty your pockets. How convenient! I bet the crooks at the theology department would love to hear that. What other tall-tales will you have for me?"

"This is no tall-tale! What I told you of my father is all true. He's a patriot and raised me to be one."

"We shall need a proof of that," the girl demanded, tapping the balustrade. "Why don't you sing about the Three Manchester Martyrs right on this spot?"

The student crumbled with embarrassment.

"I confess, I can't remember the words."

"I don't believe that bosh for a minute!" the girl defied him indignantly, wrapping her bejeweled fingers around the neck of the marble lion. "You know the words by heart. Your father would've never sent you off into the world without them."

"In that case, suit yourself, dear lady!" The student replied, abdicating and threatening at the same time. He locked his hands and began cracking his knuckles, as if they were going to play a major part in his performance. "You asked for it. Now cover your ears."

He pulled himself up from his knees in one labored motion, tore his tweed coat off, waved it above his head and began howling:

God save Ireland, cried the heroes.
God save Ireland, say we all.
Whether on the scaffold high
Or the battlefield we die.

He repeated the refrain a few times, to the indescribable delight of the girl who almost fell over the banister laughing and even greater embarrassment of his younger brother who had been standing under an elm tree all the while.

The younger boy emerged from the shadow, seized his brother by the belt loops of his trousers and pulled him out of the limelight.

"Hush, for God's sake, before the guards take you in!" he scolded the hapless singer. "You must be mad to sing such songs, in such a place and in such an abominable voice! God be my witness, this is the last time I escort you on your expeditions!" he continued reprimanding the drunken patriot. "Instead of preparing for the exams, and I must keep watch over you instead! Dissertations do not write themselves, you know. Next time I shall let the guards arrest you. A night in prison would serve you right. Wouldn't Dadaí love to hear that?"

The third student, a mutual friend of the brothers, lingered beneath the window.

"Gentle lady," he started in the most mournful tone. "Dazzling lady, I'm starving here, you see. Haven't had a morsel in my mouth in two days. I can hardly stand on my feet. What a sweet life you've got here: a fine house, a kitchen full of cooks. And what are we to do, away from home? Wouldn't you have an apple or a bread crust for a famished scholar?"

"A bread crust for a famished scholar? Would that be all? Why not ask for caviar and capers in a pastry shell?" She laughed and disappeared inside the villa.

The boy stared at the balcony longingly, sighed, preparing to leave, but the girl reappeared a few seconds later, carrying a basket covered with a linen towel.

"Here's a modest treat," she said. "Yes, my handsome stallion, you may kiss my hand, as it was done in the better times that neither one of us has been fortunate enough to witness. And in the future don't fill an empty stomach with cheap beer. It never hurts to know your limits. Now, hurry on, before you lose sight of the rest of the herd."

The basket contained freshly baked soda bread with raisins and caramelized cranberries, a triangular wedge of cheese, a few winter apples left over from last year's harvest and an assortment of Dutch chocolates wrapped in jewel-colored foil. The student thanked his benefactress with a clumsy bow and pursued his classmates as swiftly as his legs allowed.

Meanwhile, the two brothers were on their way back to Stephen's Green, their arms wrapped around each other's shoulders.

"You don't know how weary I've grown of Dublin," the eldest one whined melancholically, struggling to keep balance and clinging to his sober guide. "How I loathe the city! I drink just to forget where I am."

"Only two more years," the younger one tried to cheer him up. "Wait at least for your diploma."

"Why wait? What am I to do with a diploma? What the deuce do I need Aristotle for? You're the one with an ever-fermentin' brain, so you deal with the dead bastard. Perhaps, you'll make a scholar one day, but I'll never jump out of my rough potato skin. Nor do I desire it. I'd rather go home to Dadaí and marry at last. I go mad without my girl. Don't you know that's why I act like a lout?"

"And you do it so well," the younger one laughed. "For that alone you deserve a diploma. Recall how Dadaí told you to look after me? Did he ever fancy that the opposite would happen, that our roles would reverse?"

"Oh yes? Count the times I saved you from the bullies!"

"That was fifteen years ago. Count the times I saved you from the guards. All those nights you would've spent in jail if I hadn't been around."

"I know," the eldest boy mumbled, admitting to his inferiority, and hung his head even lower. "Every day I thank the Almighty for such a brother. Just please, don't tell Dadaí 'bout what happened tonight."

"Why shouldn't I tell him? He'd be mighty proud of you. Tonight you acted like a true patriot. You remembered the words and the tune of the song, and you were sober enough to perform it. What else can be expected of you? It's a shame Dadaí wasn't here to listen."

ONE:
Fenian Dreams
(Tulsk, Co. Rosscommon, 1910)

Brendan Malone, one of those eternally struggling Gaelic landlords, otherwise known as Potato Kings, retreated a few steps, marveling at the results of four months of grueling labor. It was a new cottage, not an enormous but a very fine one, built in the fashion that knows no time, with a foundation of large gray stones and a flat tiled roof. Soon this cottage would fill with heavy oak furniture, home-woven rugs, countless statues of saints, rifles, animal skins hung on the walls and other attributes of an intrinsically wholesome Irishman.

"Behold Dylan's face when he comes home from Dublin," spoke Brendan. "Some present waitin' for him! But he earned it, indeed. Recall how many times the damned professors threatened to kick him out? Yet he survived those dolts."

Thaddeus McCluskey, a neighbor and a tested friend of the past twenty-some years, was standing nearby, rubbing his bruised knuckles with a kind of exhausted delight.

"At last, Dylan and Caitlin can marry and quit whinin'. That'll be the loudest, dirtiest day in Roscommon, I swear. What else can you wish for?"

"For the Renwicks to vanish!" Brendan replied without hesitation. "Their bloody mansion is an eyesore. Or am I the only one who thinks so? You can see their weathercock from ten miles away. Wouldn't it please me to see the place burnt to the ground—with the whole family inside! Last Sunday I clashed with William at the market. I looked past him, but he caught me by the suspenders, pulled me aside and started tellin' me, for the tenth time, of his days in South Africa, and of Her Majesty's generosity, and of the terrible scars on his legs, and of the shiny medals he had pinned to his uniform. I've never come so close to strikin' him, I swear. He invited me to go golfin' with him. I'll show him golfin'! I'll find a hard potato and send it flyin' straight into William's eye with a shovel."

The Renwicks had been living in Tulsk for seven years now, having moved there shortly after Queen Victoria's death, but Brendan still had not reconciled with their presence. Each summer the patriarch of the family, a veteran of the Boer War, would build new additions to his house, gradually turning it into the most formidable edifice in the village, overshadowing the clay cottages of Irish families that had lived there for half a century. Mr. Renwick's spent his unlimited leisure at Roscommon Golf Club in the shade of sycamores, beechs and whitethorns. His most impressive possession was a Mors automobile, the 1904 model, imported straight from France. It had leather seats and red wood siding. Not many men in Roscommon owned such playthings. Of course, Mr. Renwick did not drive the automobile himself. Pushing the pedals was too much exertion on his maimed legs. He had a personal chauffeur driving him around.

"Why should I keep payin' a pint of blood in taxes each year for this pitiful patch of soil?" Brendan continued raging. "I can't recall a worse year. The crops failed again, six horses got struck by some illness, I have two sons studyin' in Dublin, a third of my tenants haven't paid rent since January, but the tax letters keep comin'! And the news is always the same: *Mr. Malone, we are pleased to inform you of a tax increase in the upcoming year.* Can you blame me for bein' just a wee tad bitter?"

Having fallen into a state of effervescent indignation, Brendan found it difficult to stop. Thaddeus regretted having asked his friend that perilously open-ended question: *What else can you wish for?* Had Thaddeus known it would set off such an avalanche of grievances, he would have kept his mouth shut.

"Ah, and Damian Pembroke!" Brendan gasped, having remembered another grudge. "Another pudgy cat I'd like to strangle. His plot is ten times bigger than mine, and the soil's ten times better. Plant a handful of rocks there, and in a few months you'll get first-sort wheat, honest to God! And does he ever set his foot on that land? Not that I recall. He just sits in Belfast and makes his overseer write letters once a month, as long as his tenants pay rent on time. And I stay here through all four seasons, like a bloody idiot. Not a moment's rest!"

Brendan's eyes exuded a strange shining not intended for interpretation.

At forty-three, he possessed enviable health and energy. The secret was simple; he snubbed impure homemade whiskey that was popular in Roscommon. Brendan made an oath not to drink anything of uncertain origin, not even in the moments of most pressing desperation, for he had seen too many of his childhood friends go into premature graves. Even those who were fortunate to have lived past thirty-five sported perpetually bloated faces and crimson eyes.

"I wouldn't be caught dead with my snout down the gutter!" Brendan said, resting his broad hand over his heart.

He prized cleanliness, though he had solemnly denounced formal suits, hats, gloves, ties, pocket watches, all of which he called "Saxon whims". The feeble sun yellowed his skin every summer, making it almost the same color as his hair.

He took immense pride in his iron muscles and swore that physical labor was a question of masculinity, that neither wealth nor social standing had anything to do with it. No, he was far nobler and better than Damian Renwick, for he served the land he owned.

In spring, as soon as the last patches of snow would disappear, Brendan would throw his coat on the steamy soil and join the field workers. In his presence nobody dared complaining about fatigue.

"Move!" he would yell, more for the pleasure of hearing his own voice than for the motivation of others.

The tenants worshipped Brendan and prayed for the Almighty to extend his life by another three hundred years or so. Compassionate landlords make for a rare species. As a member of the Land League, Brendan sheltered the evicted from other estates in his modest domain in exchange for seasonal work. Instead of fleeing to America or England in desperation in hopes of finding employment at factories, the displaced farmers could turn to Mr. Malone. He would give them lodging, and they would work his fields and tend to his livestock. This arrangement would spare them the ordeal of leaving their native country. Brendan subscribed to a somewhat unfashionable idea that the Irish should stay in Ireland. Diaspora has its benefits, but not when it is dictated by destitution. Ireland was becoming known as a barren nest in which future refugees hatched. This vision of his former compatriots disembarking in New York, emaciated and ragged, made Brendan's neck burn. He considered it great honor to shoulder temporary inconveniences if it meant preventing another Irish family from leaving the country. If he heard rumors of someone pondering emigration, he would immediately rush to save that poor soul.

"Do not leave Roscommon," he would implore. "Come, work for me instead. Hardships will pass, and some day you shall be happy you stayed."

Thus, the number of tiny clay hovels behind his house increased each year. He helped build and repair those hovels himself. By the age of thirty he had mastered the basic principles of carpentry and could lay bricks in his sleep.

Towards the end of December each year, Brendan would succumb to another wild onslaught of generosity. He even maintained a record of all the tenants' children and handed out presents to them on Christmas. Few things in this world are sweeter than wearing the crown of a merciful patriarch.

Generally, Brendan Malone made an impression of an amiable, reliable fellow, the sort that an occasional passer-by would ask to light a smoking pipe or give directions to the Roscommon town. Two things could dim his smile: a headache and the sound of the British accent. The latter, however, could not be held against a Republican. His hostility towards the monarchy was just as inevitable as primary sin and required neither cruelty nor malice.

Brendan had arrived at his own version of absolute truth without particular guidance from others. Before he even knew how to read, he became enchanted by a book of Celtic myths upon which he stumbled in the attic accidentally. The book clearly was not purchased by his father. It must have been left behind by the previous owner. Decades later, already being a grown man, Brendan would openly proclaim that book more holy and inspirational than the Bible. And while he was still a child, those ivory pages, with fantastical illuminated images straight from the book of Kells, comprised three quarters of his universe. Brendan would stare at his still nameless idols, waiting for them to rise from the page and initiate him into their adventures. Eventually, he learned that the boy in the armor was called Cúchulainn, and the stern-eyed old man was called Finn McCumhail, and that they both protected their land from invaders.

When Brendan declared that he wanted to devote his life to the same cause, nobody challenged his decision. His father was a wan, drowsy philistine, who looked and behaved the same in the state of sobriety or drunkenness, who had no interesting stories to tell and who barely remembered the names of his seven children or recognized their faces. The realization of his father's meagerness brought Brendan considerable shame, the very shame that later became the fuel for his adolescent fantasies.

Like most small Irish landlords, Brendan had some Saxon blood in his veins and would gladly sacrifice twenty years of his life to "purify" his heritage. On his better days, when he did not dread embarrassment before himself, Brendan attempted to recite the Lord's Prayer in Gaelic. On his worst days, he searched for ways to punish himself for not knowing the language better. He would curse himself in the third person, imitating a British accent, but then, shortly after, he would return to practicing Gaelic.

Brendan is ainm dom. Ta bhaile agam, agus is maith sin.

Brendan is my name. I have a home, and that's good.

His inner litany did not progress far beyond that point. Granted, it did not amount to much, not even a solid beginning, but it was better than nothing at all.

When the bilingual newspaper *An Claidheamh Soluis*, a Sword of Light, first came out in 1899, Brendan bought a subscription dutifully but very soon caught himself reading mostly the English versions of the articles. Appalled by this realization, he dropped the subscription altogether. Alas, it was too late for him to master the language of his ancestors. Roscommon was not the most advantageous place for linguistic pursuits. One needed to be born either in one of the Gaeltacht regions in the west of Ireland or in Dublin. The language could be learned from Galway peasants or city scholars. There was no middle ground.

Using the scant resources available to him, Brendan attempted to educate himself, drawing his own conclusions, however distorted, without anyone to correct him. From old newspaper clippings and outdated textbooks lifted from the bookcase at the local church, he had learned about the heroes of the bygone century, of the Wolfe Tones, the Young Irelanders and the first Fenians, men who were not discouraged by repeated defeats. After yet another botched campaign, the survivors would reconvene.

Without even washing the dust and the sweat off their bodies, they would take out their lap harps, fiddles, pipes, flutes, drums and dance away, burrowing holes in the ground with their heels, kiss their women, punch and shove their children. They died with a conscience no less clear than those who never spilt a drop of blood. Recall Theobald Wolfe Tone! How gently, almost innocently his eyes gazed in the intervals between battles.

Brendan Malone aspired to be another Wolfe Tone, but no serious engagement was in sight. To his infinite frustration, a meaty opportunity never transpired. Brendan had simply been born in the wrong half of the 19th century. Ireland, exhausted by the vain sporadic rebellions here and there, seemed incapable of an organized revolution.

Such inactivity would have made any man gnaw his fists with impatience. All patriotic feats that Brendan had planned for himself throughout his adolescence had culminated a few skirmishes with English civilians. Nobody died, but many cursed right and left. As Brendan grew, he abandoned those juvenile pranks and started encouraging his comrades to do the same.

"It is all but a short and straight road for a long stay in a British jail. God only knows when our time will come."

Perhaps he did not receive as much from Mars as he wanted. Venus, on the other hand, treated him more generously. After a few years of complete carelessness to which every young man is entitled, Brendan married Máirín Ó Faoláin, the prettiest girl in Tulsk, whose father also owned an enviable plot of land. That alliance brought him two sons Dylan and Hugh.

Even after twenty-three years of marriage, Máirín still caught herself smitten by Brendan in the most foolish, adolescent manner. Persistent in all his goals, he had taken her by a straightforward assault shortly after her fifteenth birthday. Because such raw youth kept Máirín from having high expectations, because such a rapid leap from virginity to maternity left her no time for pondering, dreaming or doubting, she did not suffer from any disappointment. Sometimes she giggled with pleasure, thinking how imposing her husband looked on horseback with his collar unfastened and a whip in his hand. Máirín's love, if not particularly profound, was unquestionably sincere. Such happiness, ingenuous and solid, can only be conceived in an open space, where fields roll like waves of green velvet.

Most of the time, Brendan was no marvel of gallantry. Domestic diplomacy in any form was yet another "Saxon whim." In disputes, he rarely condescended to reasoning with Máirín and usually limited his arguments to the same negligent word: "Si-lence."

While cursing, he took no pity on his throat. Some of the phrases he coined burst with such poetic flavor that W. B. Yeats himself would have gladly annexed them to his vocabulary. In moments of extreme vexation, Brendan lowered his yelling down to a whisper. Máirín had learned fairly early in their marriage that it was a sign to remove herself from her husband's view.

In the moments of contentment—and they were not by any means infrequent—Brendan would hum courting ditties and wink at her across the table. He could seize her by the forearms suddenly, make her sit on his knee and feed her from his hand or kiss her like few men kiss their wives after over twenty years of marriage. Those caresses erased from her memory all his previous offenses.

What would she not forgive her husband! Everything about Brendan struck her as endearing: his waywardness, his clumsy eloquence, his passion for whistle-dancing. Shoves mixed with kisses, curses with jokes, how could a woman grow bored? Máirín thought herself to be uncommonly fortunate. Not once did she regret choosing Brendan over the more reserved and grounded Thaddeus McCluskey who had also courted her.

The two men had not always been friends. In their youth, back in the 1880's, they had nearly shot each other over Máirín.

Eventually, Thaddeus' anger cooled down and he reconciled with Brendan's victory. And now, almost a quarter of a century later, they were preparing to merge pedigrees.

"But what 'bout Hugh?" Thaddeus asked suddenly, rummaging inside the canvas bag in search for supper. "Will you leave your youngest one without a graduation gift?"

Brendan cracked his wrist with an air of apathy.

"What can I give him? Don't you know my Hugh by now? He doesn't dwell on this earth and or even up there." He pointed at the grape-colored clouds gathering over the hill. "God only knows where he dwells. That lad's head is screwed on in a most peculiar way. Everyone thinks so, not only me. He keeps mumblin' 'bout that Plato or Pluto, and he then lapses into rage when nobody understands him. Don't you know? Last year over Christmas he yanked a tuft of his own hair out b'cause I couldn't help him with Latin. We were all sittin' by the fire, waitin' for the wren boys to come by, and he was hidin' in the corner, hunched over his books. Have you seen his back lately? It's arched like a fishin' hook! He's already got a hook for a nose, and now he's got another one growin' between his shoulder blades. Then you wonder why he's never been with a woman! I've strong doubts that he pines for his home. Believe me, Hugh doesn't stir half the trouble his brother does in college, but he gives me twice the worry."

"Ah, don't agitate yourself," Thaddeus attempted to pacify him. "How old is Hugh? Twenty-one? Well, he got 'nough time to get his wits together. 'Cyclopedias and other bosh—all shall pass like a childhood illness. Believe it or not, my Donnie went through the same whims. Now look at him! Is he not a gem of good sense? But then who knows? It may not be so dreadful to have a scholar in the family."

"Perhaps…" Brendan mumbled, blotting the blood from his knuckles. "All I know is that every time I open my mouth 'round Hugh, I feel like a perfect idiot. I can't debate French thinkers with him, you see. Is that my fault, with the sort of father we had? No, wait. I do recall some tutors swarm 'round the house. But they left soon. I was seven or eight then. I still don't know how I learned to read. Call it a miracle. Our Dadaí was an utter goon, dull as a tree stump. So, I swore that none of that would ever happen to my lads. No, they would be schooled properly. Surely, bein' a star-struck fool that I am, I took all the money I had, borrowed some here and there, just to send them both to college. Everyone told me 'twas a rotten idea, but I did not listen. No, sir, I had glorious visions! And here I am, unable to speak to my own son."

"Oh, you did right by your boys," Thaddeus continued to reassure his friend. "I would've done the same for Donnie, had I possessed the means. Now your Hugh shall see the world."

"And what's the matter wi' this world?" Brendan shook his arms before him. "Do tell! Why do men flee from it? Some even go across the ocean. True, I haven't seen much besides these hills and fields, but I doubt there's much out there that's worth more. Those banks full of fat cats who strip us down bear with taxes? Those coal mines in Doncaster? Those stenchin' factories? Oh, I saw one in Dublin and thought I'd go deaf. Our men work inside those hell pits. Yes, they pour there from Leitrim, from Roscommon. For what, dare I ask? I keep my tenants happy. Not a soul can deny that. I let them stay on my patch of land, however small and barren it may be. I don't chase them off if they cannot pay rent, at least not at once. We've all got an honest arrangement here, no? So why isn't it good 'nough for Hugh?"

Brendan sunk his teeth into his lower lip. Thaddeus watched him with silent sympathy. He knew it was useless to console his friend any further. Hugh had always been a tender subject for Brendan.

Thaddeus himself was not a pensive sort. He rarely preoccupied his mind with hatred for the British or with worries about his children's future. The past was intended for oblivion, and the future—for obscurity.

Thaddeus turned his eyes to the wavy path that pushed into the horizon and suddenly jerked his friend by the sleeve.

"Look, isn't that your lad?"

Brendan leaped to his feet, peering into the road, and in the orange light of the sun, in about quarter of a mile away, saw a young man.

"By God, 'tis him! Dylan!"

The young man was close enough to hear his name. He speeded up his pace and tore the cap off his head.

"Dadaí!"

Every time Brendan looked at his eldest son, he needed to summon all his willpower to refrain from pounding himself in the chest before the rest of the mortal fathers.

Dylan Malone belonged to that fortunate type that flourished in eastern Connaucht. Traveling from Loughlynn to Stokestown, one can always count on meeting a man with hair like old copper coins and eyes like boiled spinach. The whiteness of Dylan's skin seemed invincible to the sun. Only in the moments of agitation did blush come out on his high cheekbones in large brick-orange patches. And he got excited easily. It took no more than a joke, even the stupidest, to have him rolling on the ground. Truly, Dylan was a gem, if not of intelligence than at least of good nature. He pranced at the sight of his father, who immediately gathered him in a gusty ursine embrace.

"Look who's home at last!" Brendan roared and suddenly pushed his son away, bursting into laughter, not of benevolent but of mocking nature, which puzzled and alarmed the boy.

"What's wrong, Dadaí?"

Brendan pointed to Dylan's clothes.

"No, you tell me what's wrong," he shook his head disapprovingly. "Come, turn 'round. Holy Christ, what have they done to my son? Lacquered shoes? Since when? I won't say a word 'bout that coat of yours. It was tailored for a scarecrow. We'll put it on the straw man who keeps the birds away from the garden. But that round hat, and the tie—what the devil? Tell me, lad, you like wearin' a noose 'round your neck?"

Dylan, always agonizingly sensitive to his father's criticism, found himself on the verge of panic.

"It's not my fault, I swear!" he began ranting, waving his arms in self-defense. "What was I to do, Dadaí? They all dress in this fashion nowadays."

"Perhaps in Dublin they do," Brendan carried on without any intention of showing mercy, "but you're on my property now, so you live by my rules. No ribbons or bows of any sort. That's an order. Relate that to your brother. Speakin' of the devil, where the hell is Hugh? Or did you lose him 'long the road?"

"He stopped by the house first, to give Mamaí a kiss."

"Why am I not astonished?" Brendan muttered and rolled his eyes. "Kissin' Mamaí. Now *that's* a sacred ritual!"

Indeed, for Hugh, greeting his mother after a lengthy separation was nothing short of a sacrament, one that he preferred to perform without the distraction of other family members. With all three men in the house, it was not easy for Máirín to squeeze a word or a kiss in. Her light high-pitched voice that had not changed much since she was a girl would drown in the howling and the stamping of feet. Like most women of her station, she was usually seen but not heard.

"The tenants told me you'd be here with Uncle Tad," Dylan continued, tugging at his tie frantically, struggling to pull it off his neck. "Plasterin' another house? More tenants, eh? Who'll be movin' here?"

"A certain young scholar," Thaddeus replied, watching self-complacently as the young man's eyes widened. "Consider it a graduation gift from your father and me, a token of parental blessin'. So, even if you rethink marryin' Caitlin, too late now."

Thaddeus suddenly locked his arm around Dylan's neck and pulled him aside, hissing in his ear, "Rest assured, I know all 'bout Caitlin's trip to Dublin four month ago, so don't bother tellin' me otherwise."

The young man glanced at Thaddeus fearfully.

"You know, Uncle Tad? I mean, Mr. McCluskey. How did you find out?"

"Why, the entire county knows, even though nobody says a word. Caitlin is with child. Such secrets cannot be kept forever, dear boy. Don't pull away from me now, you brazen piglet. Lucky for you, I'm not the sort of father who'd break your neck for such deeds. God knows I've been in your shoes. That's why I'll settle for a warnin'. Better make haste with marriage."

Dylan blushed and bowed obediently, his body language being reasonably consistent with the magnitude of his transgression. Kneeling, penitent breast-beating or hair-tearing would have been excessive, at least with Mr. McCluskey. With him Dylan did not even need to apologize.

"You have my word, sir."

"And I'll hold you to it!" Thaddeus promised sternly, releasing Dylan from his grip. "Off with you, piglet. I, too, better take my leave now. Go home, scream at my wife, perhaps."

"Scream at Mrs. McCluskey?" Dylan gasped fearfully. "What has she done this time?"

"'Tis what she hasn't done!" Thaddeus replied, flexing his fists. "I thought there would be dinner in my sack. No such luck! My wife means to starve me to death. A long day we've had, much too long…"

On this note Thaddeus parted with his friend and his future son-in-law.

Struggling to absorb the news of impending fatherhood, Dylan stepped inside the house, leaned over the windowsill and stroked the walls on which the paint was still moist.

"How odd, only a few months ago the hill was barren," he muttered and turned to his father. "Dadaí, you have no equals. To build such a castle! And where did you get the money? Confess, whom did you rob?"

"Nobody, 'pon my soul!" Brendan replied, raising both hands in the air.

"All right then: what did you sell?"

"Nothin'! I'm tellin' you the truth. By God, why must you get so nosey over matters that aren't of your concern? Thaddeus and I had a few coins saved up, so we kept hush 'bout it. And what else can we spend it on if not our children? You'll be doin' the same for your own brats once they come. Let's find that brother of yours."

***

The first thing Brendan heard upon crossing the threshold was his wife's sobbing. Máirín never neglected a chance to shed a few tears, especially when she had an audience. Years only enhanced the inclination. There was nothing more habitual for Brendan than to see his wife's eyes fill with salty moisture. That neither vexed nor touched him any longer. He told himself that it was one of those mysterious womanly rituals, and gave her the right to cry for her own pleasure, for whatever reason. And is there a reason more suitable than the children's return?

Without knowing Máirín's temperament, one could easily imagine that this woman was welcoming her sons after five years of war instead of just a few month of schooling. Hugh, her favorite, kept stroking her back.

"There, Mamaí, everyone's alive and well. Save your tears for the next funeral. But look, here's Dylan. You haven't kissed him yet."

Brendan rolled his eyes at this sissy behavior.

"Here she goes again, kissin' and cuddlin'!"

But Máirín had already forgotten about Hugh and fluttered over to her eldest son, who needed mother's caresses just as much, though he was hesitant to ask for them in the presence of his stern father.

24

"Dylan! Why so lean, so pale?" she cackled. "I prayed to Jesus, Mary and Joseph you weren't ill. Did they not feed you there? Or did those accursed professors torture you?"

"Perhaps, they didn't torture him 'nough!" Brendan replied only half-jokingly. "Blast you, woman! Don't you see what your love's doin' to my sons? You're robbin' the country of men! No wonder His Bloody Majesty King Edward is still at our throats!"

"I don't care," Máirín confessed, throwing her head back with maternal obstinacy, "as long as my little ones are by my side. And how can you even think of war? Look at their faces—pure cherubs!"

And to confirm her words, she pinched the youngest one on the cheek even though there was not much flesh to pinch.

Hugh Malone was not all that terrible looking, and if people said otherwise, it was only because his appearance seemed so foreign for Irish midlands. Cursed with naturally olive skin that turned green during mild bout of anemia, he was also taller than the other men in his family, thinner in the waist, narrower in the shoulders. Perhaps, a society that did not prize physical strength so much would have treated Hugh more benevolently, but in his native land he did not enjoy half of his brother's popularity. More than that, Dylan's conformity to the canons of Gaelic masculine beauty made Hugh stand out even more.

Had Hugh been born half a century earlier, he would have been branded a changeling. The villagers would have said that Brendan's real son had been kidnapped by evil sprites and replaced with this odd creature.

"He resembles a Jew," the lads in the village whispered among themselves, careful not to be heard by Dylan, who would not think twice to crack a few skulls in defense of his baby brother.

One time, a certain overly compassionate female sighed. "Poor, homely Hugh... To have shoulders like a lad of thirteen, such a heavy dropping nose that bleeds for no reason at all, such scrawny legs that neither run fast nor jump high. What shall become of him? What woman will have him?"

People had yet another reason for giving him suspicious stares, and that was his obvious reluctance to blend into the world from which he had sprung. Hugh rarely opened his mouth, and that very silence made him stand out from the crowd. He did not drink—whiskey made him dizzy. He did not smoke—tobacco made him nauseous. He did not fight—the sight of blood disturbed him. Above all, he always wore that expression of internal unrest and discontentment. Something alien always slipped into his moves and his talk.

The village lads had conspired to walk clumsily, stamping their feet and swinging their arms, proudly bashing all concepts of gracefulness. Hugh was the only one who did not follow the custom. Feeble as he was, he trod with his narrow shoulders turned out, his thin neck stretched and his sharp chin lifted. Of course, the villagers concluded that he paid no respect to the old custom. He was tall already and strove to appear even taller. His height was only physical advantage over others, so he made sure to exploit it to the fullest.

There also existed unwritten law against speaking pure English. When somebody did not swallow and blend certain sounds, others would notice it immediately and start rumbling. Dylan Malone could not wait to shed the polished pronunciation that his teachers imposed upon him and which choked him like the satin tie they made him wear. Immediately after crossing the threshold of his father's house, Dylan would dive blissfully into the heaven of bad grammar. Hugh, on the other hand, did not suffer from nostalgia for the provincial Roscommon accent. After four years in college he sounded almost like a native Dubliner from a relatively affluent circle. At times, it was difficult to believe that Hugh and Dylan originated from the same family.

For the purpose of mere self-preservation, Hugh preferred to keep silent among his compatriots, who were willing to tolerate only the minimal amount of scholastic knowledge. Most small landlords of Brendan's rank were content if their children could scribble complete sentences and knew just enough Latin to understand the Mass. Sending children away to the city to learn all the sciences and foreign philosophies bordered on extravagance. Brendan, laden with his own unrealized ambitions, became seduced by the notion of his children receiving a solid Gaelic schooling. He grasped at the promise of University College Dublin, which was to educate Irish Catholic boys in their native tradition.

Partially blinded, Brendan did not perceive the other edge of the sword, namely that Dublin was an excellent place for a Roscommon boy to become anglicized. Half of the faculty professors at University College were English. Eion MacNeill and Douglas Hyde, the founders of the Gaelic League, were not the only ringmasters in the cultural arena in the city still thoroughly drenched in Anglicism. Brendan had not thought that by sending his children to Dublin, he would be dunking them in a sea of English influences and temptations that they would not necessarily be able to resist.

The possibility that one or both of his sons may not choose the path of Irish nationalism did not occur to Brendan. No doubt, they would both emerge fluent in Gaelic and devoted to the Cause wholeheartedly. Brendan had already compiled a list of organizations they would join after graduation, including the Land League and the Republican Brotherhood. No other outcome was possible, not with his children. Armed with their knowledge, they would join the new crop of native Irish elite.

Everyone in Tulsk knew that the Malone brothers attended University College, and everyone smiled approvingly each time Brendan came to a gathering and shook his head with affected distress.

"What am I to do with Dylan?" he would lament, making sure that he had plenty of listeners. "He ran away again, the devil's brat! They found him in a pub, just before the exams. Would you believe it? His noggin isn't made to hold sciences. I wonder after whom he takes."

And all of Brendan's friends would begin consoling him.

"Who needs those bloody sciences?"

One day one of his neighbors said, "Half of what an Irishman needs to know he learns in battle. But when was that last battle worthy of a mention? That's why we got a whole generation of fools and lazybones."

On the horseback nobody surpassed Dylan, who had been in the saddle since the age of five. Watching his son galloping in the yard, Brendan would cry out, "Well done, chieftain!"

Chieftain! That nickname would make any man with minimal sense and taste cringe, but Brendan, blinded by ambition and intoxicated with paternal pride, was hardly in a state to reason. The nickname never failed to produce the desired effect on Dylan. The boy lived only to earn it and hear it. He would spur his horse and throw his head back, laughing to the sun.

"Behold his posture!" Brendan would exclaim. "What a grip he has!"

More than once Dylan ended up on the ground facedown, his mouth filled with dust and tiny rocks. Yet each time some instinct forbade him to cry. Brendan would dismount from his horse and stand over his son without any intention of helping him up.

"Is your head still on?" he would ask nonchalantly.

"I think I broke my leg, Dadaí," Dylan would whimper. "Hurts like hell, swear God—

"Ah, don't fret. 'Twas not your fault. Now, get back on that horse. There! You'll be a chieftain, I see that!"

Intoxicated with fatherly pride, Brendan would turn to his youngest son who, was still clinging to his mother's skirt, observing his father with awe in his enormous Semitic eyes.

"And you, what shall we make of you?"

"Don't touch the baby, Bren!" Máirín would warn him. "Hugh's still mine."

"Oh, be silent! Don't meddle in my plans, woman. You gave birth to him and you nursed him. Your work's done. What else do you want? Want him to grow up a whimperin' pup, eh? Oh, he'll be a Fenian too. I'll make him one, even if I must shatter him first to smithereens and then rebuild him anew! Granted, he'll never be like his brother, but there's still hope for Hugh. Let my eldest be a chieftain and my youngest a bard. A bard isn't terrible either."

The Creator had not sent Hugh into the world without blessings altogether. By the age of seventeen he had developed a tolerable voice, something between a tenor and a high baritone. To his father's dismay, most of Hugh's favorite songs came from other countries, not Ireland. He could sing English, French and German melodies with complete abandonment, but not Celtic ones.

From where did such love of foreign art stem? What possessed Hugh to go to the New Year's masquerade as a Turk, wearing those unheard of eastern trousers? Dylan, who every year dressed as a peasant of the Great Famine times, told his family about the noise stirred by Hugh's costume, not suspecting how deeply the story bewildered and disturbed his father. Brendan never confronted Hugh about the Turkish incident — it would be silly to scold the boy for his choice of costume — but his mind wandered involuntarily back to the folk stories of changelings. Perhaps, his youngest son was of Mohammedan blood after all. That would certainly explain the swarthy skin, the curly black hair, the crooked nose and the owl's eyes.

Still, Hugh's strangest quality was his relationship with the fair sex. In that respect, he differed from his older brother the most. For

Dylan, love between a man and a woman never transcended the boundaries of flesh, that healthy, primitive drive that inevitably leads to parenthood. He was engaged to the girl that Dadaí had pointed out to him. Brendan had shouldered all the negotiations. Dylan's job was to make the official proposal and not look like a complete idiot. Dadaí could not have picked a more perfect bride for him. Caitlin McCluskey was fresh-faced, sweet, compliant, reassuringly inexperienced and, above all, willing to give in every time he felt the urge. Such an arrangement satisfied him to the brim of his cap and beyond. Other aspects of love remained out of his intellectual range. Simplicity is next to godliness.

Hugh, however, held his own view of Eve's daughters, to his father's infinite displeasure. The insane boy was not even a skirt chaser, which at least would have been understandable and natural for his age, but rather a skirt worshipper! He took it into his head to admire women, to endow them with noble traits and talents.

Sometimes Hugh smiled at the quiet village girls, but with purely fraternal tenderness, almost pity, reserving more intense feelings for the willful, freedom-loving women, of which there was no shortage in Dublin. The city burst with Amazons and Bohemians. They were not always the prettiest or the most virtuous ones, but they held to their own principles and ambitions, which Brendan found laughable, and Hugh found breathtaking.

The young man often tried to envision his future wife: impeccably rational yet not deprived of imagination, full of passions and wishes yet able to bridle them at a will at any moment. Through the veil of his early carnal fantasies he saw her white narrow back that did not slouch even in the moments of deepest grief, a proud head that did not bow save over some brilliant book, thin dark lips folded in a philosophical, all-knowing smile, lucid gray eyes equally eager to absorb and radiate light.

At the age of nineteen Hugh had become infatuated with Isabel McCormack, a divine girl who spouted vertigo-inducing sneers, the stepdaughter of a Polish nobleman Count Markiewicz. All respectable matrons of Dublin trembled at the very sound of her name and applied all efforts to shield their sons from her, for she was the most notorious menace to everything proper, even worse than Maud Gonne herself! Isabel could easily appear at a formal reception escorted by two stout peasants dug up from the depths of Connemara. She could quarrel with her mother's forty-year old friends and on the same breath address the cook as "sir." She could be morose and uncompromising. She could be impetuous and tender. She could curse in Polish and Ukrainian – a custom she adopted from her stepfather who never was particularly careful with words. She also knew most of Horace and Virgil by heart.

Amazingly enough, the girl took a genuine interest in Hugh. From her superhumanly charitable mother she had inherited the hobby of taking young underprivileged scholars under her wing. One evening she even invited Hugh to her house to sing at a party when the Count's relatives arrived from Warsaw on a visit. Hugh, ecstatic over the chance to entertain such a refined audience, stood in the middle of the living room and sang his favorite musical piece, *Green Sleeves*. When the girl heard the melody with the lyrics of Henry VIII in it, her alabaster face clouded. She took Hugh by the arm, led him aside and said, "Your voice is certainly better than your brother's. You are a singer, right enough, but you are certainly no patriot."

"I never claimed to be a patriot," Hugh stated without blinking. "Nor do I aspire to be one. With any luck, I can become another mediocre scholar. After my death I will not leave an independent Celtic empire, just a few obscure dissertations. This is the most I endeavor to take away from my college years."

As it turned out, Isabel harbored a profound affinity for the Republicans, as her birth father was a member of the Fenian Brotherhood. Hugh was not that self-denying Cúchulainn for which she had mistaken him initially. Personal intellectual fulfillment, as he confessed that evening, interested him far more than his country's freedom.

"Yes, I am an unabashed bookworm, bred for a sterile academic environment," Hugh continued. "I've never fired a rifle. I am half-blind in my left eye. The sight and the smell of blood terrify me. Ireland is better off without a soldier like me."

Hugh fully expected that such a candid confession from him would ruin his chances with the count's stepdaughter. Of course, he could have lied to her or at least attempted to lie. He could have told her that he had every intention of joining the Brotherhood. Perhaps, that would have won him a few waltzes with her on the dance floor or even a few kisses. But by then he was too smitten with Isabel to invent a convincing fable. Infatuation made him unflinchingly honest. With a mixture of pride, resignation and sorrow, he prepared to leave her mansion, but the girl followed him to the antechamber, squeezed his hands and swore that his political preferences made no difference to her, that such candor as his had become a rarity. Her intellectual appetite was piqued as it had not been in months, and she wished to continue their dialogue very much.

The two of them spent a few glorious evenings walking arm in arm down Grafton Street, discussing the philosophers of the Enlightenment era, exchanging terse, sincere compliments and eventually kisses. It astonished Hugh to discover that the ritual of kissing, that he had previously considered a daunting, unreachable to him privilege, in reality did not require any preliminary practice. It was merely another movement of the lips, spontaneous and natural, much like talking or smiling, only far more pleasurable. For that one did not even need to be handsome, accomplished or sought-after. Suddenly, the mystery crumbled, leaving a slight tingling in the corners of the mouth and warm tension below the belt.

"How I envy your freedom, Isabel," Hugh sighed, knowing in advance that their intimacy would not progress beyond those few kisses. "You do whatever you please, and your parents approve invariably."

She shook her exquisitely sculpted head, making the crystal chandelier earrings jingle, and suddenly leaned against Hush's narrow, underdeveloped chest, which nearly brought on another wheezing attack. Her fingers dug into his bony sides. Such closeness was all too much for his agitated nerves. The tension below the belt was growing more noticeable. He may have had trouble with his lungs, but other parts of his body functioned enviably well. Could this be? He, the village weakling, the swarthy freak, was holding the most enigmatic and coveted woman in Dublin. He could still taste the rose-flavored pomade that she used to tint her lips. The discussion and the kissing had indeed taken place. What would his classmates at University College say?

"My darling Hugh," Isabel began with a hint of melancholy, "have you ever wondered about the price of such freedom? Should you lose faith in your principles some day, you can always blame your father, or your parish priest or any other oppressive patriarchal figure for having imposed them upon you. In perfectly clear conscience you can proclaim yourself a victim of another person's deceit. And I, who had never tasted of familial oppression in her life, whom can I hold accountable? Oh, it's a frightening thing to be your own judge and your own executioner. There's nobody to beg for mercy. That is precisely why I avoid giving myself to any one cause wholeheartedly. You may have noticed that I give out plenty of presents, but very few promises. Do not let my kisses go to your head, dear Hugh. I simply couldn't restrain myself. All this talk about Descartes made my blood bubble. Say, if one day I meet a man worthy of becoming my idol, and if that man does something abominable, truly unforgivable, whom will I blame then?"

"Does it mean that you'll denounce our friendship if I stumble or disappoint you?" Hugh asked, wondering if that would be a suitable time to release her from his embrace. He knew he could not prolong and exploit that heavenly moment indefinitely. Isabel saved him from the necessity to initiate the break and slipped from his arms as swiftly as she enveloped herself in them.

Her eyebrows, always remarkably mobile and expressive, suddenly contracted and froze, which communicated earnestness and exclusive confidence.

"Only if you forfeit your free will," she declared. "I do not care on whose side you fight, or if you choose not to fight at all. If you let others turn you into their puppet, then I shall disown you for certain. Of course, I shall cry for a very long time."

"I shall never give you such cause for tears," Hugh vowed, knowing that after this promenade with Isabel he would never be able to return to those voiceless, intimidated female creatures waiting for him back at Roscommon. "As long as I breathe, I shall continue doing things my way and pay for it. I'll take the most crooked roads if they'll lead me where I desire to be!"

Having adapted to life in Dublin, Hugh longed for his father's home less and less. Brendan sensed that, yet he welcomed his son with all the warmth he could muster.

"Relieved to be finished with the studies, are you? Still readin' Plato?"

"No, Dadaí, I haven't read Plato in two years. The Ancient Greeks had never fascinated me. My focus is on the French Enlightenment—namely Descartes."

"And that Descartes fellow will feed you, right?"

"Perhaps, Descartes himself won't, but something else surely will." Hugh coughed, covering his mouth with his knuckles. "I have an employment situation in mind, permanent, reasonably lucrative and perfectly respectable. I'll earn enough money and buy a flat in the city for you and Mamaí. Is that fair enough?"

Brendan took a few moments to digest the images of the Mecklenburgh Street in Dublin, a district known for its vice trading. The authorities did not exert enough effort to exterminate the illicit activity, and every night hundreds of scandalously dressed love-peddlers would parade in front of the fancy shops and gourmet restaurants. The ladies catered to everyone from sailors to bankers. Decidedly, there was no need for a married middle-aged man with a strong body and a weak willpower to be exposed to such provocations. Devoted as Brendan was to his wife, he knew his limitations. Forty-three was not a good age to begin testing the steadfastness of his Catholic faith. He could not vouch that prayers could elevate him above carnal curiosity. His own brother Sean, formerly an emblem of piety, began straying from his wife of twenty years after a mere week in the city. If Sean could fall into sin so easily, it could happen to anyone. Yes, Dublin had that effect on married men.

"A flat in the city…" he echoed at last, glancing up at the ceiling. Then his gaze reverted back to his youngest son. "If that is what I wanted, I would've found the means of achievin' it by now. Don't you think?"

Hugh examined his father's crusted knuckles and the missing fingernail on the right thumb, a reminder of a brick-laying accident. Brendan was lucky the join had not been damaged. A mangled thumb is one of the worst injuries for someone who works with his hands.

"But, Dadaí, you can't walk behind the plough for the rest of your days."

"Oh, yes I can!" Brendan objected, taking offense to the implication that he was growing older and weaker. "I'm not movin' an inch from this land, and neither is Dylan. I just finished buildin' a splendid cottage for him and Caitlin. I've always dreamed of givin' such a present for my son. But where's *your* woman? You aren't preparin' for ordination, are you?"

"No fear of that, rest assured," Hugh mumbled with a twitch of an eyebrow.

Still, Brendan kept on scratching his chin suspiciously.

"That lucrative employment situation of yours…Why don't you tell me 'bout it?"

"I most certainly will, when the time is right?"

"Why can't you tell me now? You haven't been home for an hour, and you're givin' me worry already."

Fortunately, at this moment Máirín, whose eyes had dried up by then, summoned everyone to dinner in her sing-song voice.

"Sit down, children. You too, Brendan!"

When Dylan saw a huge mountain of fried fish, he trembled all over like a famished stray cat.

"What're we waitin' for? Let's assault the table! But Dadaí, please, let Hugh say Grace this time. I just love the way he does it—in Gaelic and Latin! Even the lads in college applauded at the table."

Family dinners in the Malone were a raucous affair. All efforts seemed to be directed onto one purpose: to turn the table set up by Máirín's hospitable hands into a rubbish yard for bare fish skeletons and cherry stays bombarding the empty whiskey bottles. The whiskey, of course, had been tested for purity and approved by the head of the house.

Sweet weariness added an oily glow to Brendan' face. The fiery, relentless pig-headedness retreated, giving way to rudimentary sarcasm, although his provincial accent became more obvious.

"Fancy that," he spoke, tossing his head from one shoulder to another, "the other eve'n Eion McLeod, that bundy-legged Scotsman with a windmill, asked me, 'Why don't yer lads ever play wi' mine? And why do yer men despise our men? Ain't we of the same roots? We're all Gaels, right?' And I answer, 'Why d'ye s'ppose there was a civil war in America? Don't they bow to the same President?' I swear poor Eion didn't git a word o' mine. So he stood, peepers bulgin', mouth agape, catchin' flies. I was holdin' my sides crackin'. Then, I ask, 'Why d'ye s'ppose your Petey and Mickey thrash one another dead each blessed Friday? Ain't they brothers? Ain't they of the same father? I guess, not!' I'm tellin' ye, lads..."

Again, Brendan burst out laughing, until his laughter fizzled into a faint sob, as he tapped the glass with his finger.

"What's that on the bottom? Currants? Blast that woman! Again she threw a handful o'berries in whiskey! I tole her thousan' times I hated it. It's good, pure whiskey, and those damned berries look like tiny roaches without legs. Colin O'Nevin almost choked on those. There, lads, your mother's tryin' to kill me. No wonder Christ never married! Had he been any friendlier to Mary Magdalene, he never would've reached Golgotha!"

After another few minutes of reflections, Brendan addressed Dylan, very gravely. "Tell ye the truth 'bout those Scots like McLeod. Nice men, polite men, but cowardly. True, they had Willie Wallace. But that's all they had! And us?" Brendan punched himself in the chest with such force that his teeth clang. "Each of us is like Willie. Only we don't brag 'bout it. Listen, lads! Listen to your father!"

The cheap alcoholic concoctions that had kept Dylan alive in Dublin simply could not compare to Dadaí's quality whiskey. Jut a few mouthfuls of that costly ambrosia disposed him to reminiscence. The young graduate began telling his father about John Ashley, his legendary enemy at college. Staring at the palm of his hand intently, Dylan kept bending his fingers one by one.

"So, I was beatin' and kickin' him, and he was screachin' like a bloody cur, and I kept on beatin' him... 'Twas a glorious occasion, Dadaí. You should've been there to cheer me on."

"Right 'nough." Brendan gave his eldest son a steadfast, provocative stare. "We know your kind all too well. You wouldn't harm a cat."

Dylan twitched on the bench, trying to straighten up.

"You think I'm lyin'?"

"I bet a shillin' that you're lyin'."

"Well, I bet two shillin' that I can bash your brains out, Dadaí," Dylan retaliated, taken aback by his own audacity. "You don't believe me?"

"Fair 'nough!" Brendan concluded, drumming on the tabletop. "Roll up your sleeves, spit on your fists and come outside. I haven't thrashed you in ages. Easy, lad... Dadaí loves you, whoreson that you are."

At that moment Hugh, who had limited himself to half a glass of weak apple wine that his mother put out for him exclusively, spoke up for the first time that evening.

"Dylan, where are your wits? Thrashing Dadaí! He's no longer young, and he's had too much to drink. Don't you see his condition? He can hardly stand up straight."

Brendan started wheezing like a maddened bull, pushing his knuckles into the tabletop.

"Listen to yourself! Wouldn't we like to see you twenty years from now? Take notice, lad, say that again, and I'll shoot you!"

"Promises, promises, as usual," Hugh muttered gloomily, playing with the fork, and then glanced up at his father. "Where have you been all this time, Dadaí? I've been hearing the same threat for the past twenty years."

Brendan already opened his mouth, ready to spout out another threat, but Dylan pulled him by the arm.

"Let's go, Dadaí. Thrash me instead. Don't touch Hugh."

"Indeed, why would I bother with him?" Brendan said spitefully, still peering into Hugh's gaunt face. "He'll crash from a single blow. Some fun fighin' him..."

The father and his favorite son fell over the threshold, hanging on each other. They could not wait to let their fists loose. As soon as the door slammed, the first punches and grunts were heard.

Máirín dropped her hands over her apron.

"Is this how all our dinners shall end from now on?" she asked Hugh, demanding to be comforted.

"Of course not, Mamaí," he gave her the answer that she wanted to hear. "We must humor Dadaí. After all, this is our homecoming night. You cannot expect him to be civil and proper. Once the novelty of having his whole family at the same table wears off, he will surely settle."

Dylan returned fifteen minutes later, hair tousled, left cheekbone beginning to swell. Apparently, the grapple had sobered him up a bit.

"Where's Dadaí?" Hugh asked him.

Dylan wagged his hand indefinitely.

"On the hay where I left him," he replied, still struggling to stabilize his breathing. "You were right, Hugh. Dadaí is old and drunk. His fighin' days are over. I'm the king of fist-a-cuffs now, though it took me twenty-two years to defeat him." Dylan then turned to Máirín. "Wait now, Mamaí! Where're you takin' the whiskey jar? Leave it out, I say! I'm not done drinkin' yet. Besides, I brought us company. My future brother-in-law is here."

Donnie McCluskey, named after the river Don in Yorkshire where his brave grandfather had drowned, was almost a third son to Brendan and Máirín. While Dylan and Hugh had been away at college, he frequented their parents' house. With a charming childlike immediacy he would lay his burning claws on everything that caught his eye. In this particular instant it happened to be a mangled slice of cherry pie left over from the dinner.

"You've been savin' it for me, Mrs. Malone, haven't you?" he asked with an all-knowing wink.

"Eat your fill, dear boy," Máirín said. "There's more in the kitchen. And whatever doesn't fit in your cheeks you can take home with you. How are your little ones?"

"Ravenous—all three!" Donnie boasted, tearing into the pie. "It's plain to see whom they take after. When the fourth one comes, they'll need to curb their appetites." Suddenly, Donnie realized that he had not greeted Hugh properly. "Good day, my fine scholar! Has Our Lord been kind to you?"

"Kinder than I deserve," Hugh replied. "Of course, I cannot compete with your reproductive achievements. I have no such reasons to brag."

"Ah, you will some day!" Donnie raised his index finger, giving himself a chance to swallow the cherry filling. "Alison O'Mara's still waitin'. Granted, she's no great beauty, but by God, does she have patience! What else can a poor girl do but wait—with a face like hers? The good news is that when you blow out the candles, faces don't matter. But listen to this, gents. Last night I was tossin' cards with the O'Nevin twins, and this grand idea came to me."

Donnie McCluskey was the unsurpassed king of grand ideas, a chieftain appointed by nature. Every prank turned out a success if he was in command. As his spirit matured, however, he moved onto deeds somewhat more chivalrous. When a portion of Joseph O'Mara's house had burnt down, it was Donnie who had organized a charitable collection of money from the neighborhood. The folks had instantly forgiven him the robbed fruit orchards and the hens painted green.

"What's on your mind this time?" Dylan asked. He always grasped at a chance to partake in Donnie's endeavors.

"A ride to the river. Just think! No whinin' brats, no naggin' wives. They'll manage on their own for a few days. Gents only, ten-fifteen of us. Say, in the month o' August, before the field works begin, we harness the horses, load the rifles and take off to Shannon. You're comin' with us, right?"

"No question 'bout it!" Dylan shouted. "But, for Christ's sake, don't mention guns and rifles before my Mamaí. She'll surely faint."

Donnie pressed both fists to his chest solemnly, letting his friend know that he had every intention of honoring his request, and then turned towards the youngest of the Malone brothers.

"I take it, you're comin', too?"

Hugh shut the notebook in which he had been scribbling for the past ten minutes and glanced up at Donnie.

"Regretfully, no, though, I do thank you for the invitation. I simply won't be here in August. I'm home on a short visit."

"And why is that?" Donnie asked, squinting suspiciously. "Where're you scurryin' off to?"

"To Belfast, on business," Hugh continued indulging the neighbor's curiosity as patiently as he could. "An opportunity transpired. I thought that time has come for me to start making my own living and let my poor father breathe."

"Mr. Malone seems to be breathin' well as ever."

"Precisely, he *seems* to be breathing well," Hugh corrected him. "In reality, he's choking—with guilt. Did you know that he was forced to raise rent to pay for our schooling?"

"So?" Donnie shrugged and wiped the greasy crumbs off his shirt. "Where's the tragedy? Life isn't cheapenin'. Everyone else raises rent, includin' my own father. How do you think I keep my children fed? Their number keeps growin'. I can't be kept awake at night over this. I can't deprive my own family."

Donnie's dimwittedness, which in a more evolved man could pass for blatant callousness, began wearing down Hugh's diplomacy.

"True, many landlords remain unbothered," he said, raising his voice, "but my father hates putting strain on his tenants, and I, in turn, don't cherish putting a strain on him. Do you not understand, Donnie? Dadaí would rather have a piece of his liver cut out than make his tenants pay more. I know what toll it takes on him."

Hugh was acutely aware of the contrast between his mannerisms and Donnie's. Only a year earlier he would have made another conscious effort to simplify his speech and repress his English accent acquired in Dublin. God forbid, he should be thought an urban snob or a sympathizer of the crown! That evening, however, he saw no need to continue pretending. More than that, he strove to emphasize his linguistic superiority over Donnie, purposely choosing multisyllabic words and articulating the endings.

"My father takes particular pride in being able to accommodate his tenants," Hugh continued with growing impatience. "He understands that the soil here has very little to offer to agrarian entrepreneurs. It is not such an enormous blessing after all to have a hut built on his property. The crop fails practically every other year. At least, my father can compensate for the bareness of the land by keeping the rent reasonable. I cannot continue bleeding him for the sake of my scholastic ambition. I must start paying my own way, so he can lower the rent to what it once was. Then he will sleep sounder, and so will I."

Donnie suddenly stopped gorging and covered his mouth.

"My God," he whimpered indistinctly through his fingers.

Máirín dropped her dishrag and rushed to his side.

"What's the matter, love?" she asked fearfully, taking him by the shoulders. "Did you chip a tooth? I could've sworn I removed all the cherry stays, but there's always that one that makes its way into the pie."

"It's just..." Donnie mumbled and let out a convulsive sigh. "It's just that everyone in your family is so bloody noble. I'm so moved, I'm about to cry. Ah!"

And he burst out laughing, spraying cherry-tinted saliva all over his shirt and the tablecloth. Watching him, Máirín began laughing too, shortly joined by both of her sons.

"In earnest," Donnie continued, having caught his breath, "Hugh's an odd one. He always has schemes of his own, no matter what others do. I never quite know what's on his mind."

To tantalize a compulsively breeding village idiot with one's erudition and eloquence was proving to be a less than gratifying exercise for Hugh.

Shame on me, Hugh thought. I have no right to aggravate Donnie like that. It isn't fault that he cannot tie two words together. I should rise above such pettiness. This is not an equal battle.

"Believe me, Donnie, even I don't always know what is on my mind," he said out loud, hoping to draw the attention away from his person, even though in the end his words produced the opposite effect. "My thoughts keep wandering and fermenting. Still, some basic principles remain the same. First of all, I must relieve my parents of their monetary burden. I'd like to believe that my education was not in vain. There is nothing unnatural about one's desire to make a living through the work of one's intellect."

Donnie squinted in confusion, deliberating how to formulate a response. He did not know how to interpret Hugh's last statement, whether to feel insulted. Were those words intended as a subtle sneer, a stab at Donnie's dependency upon his parents? In the McCluskey family it was not considered shameful for children to accept handouts from the older generation. Both Donnie and his sister always relied on their father to satisfy their needs and repaid him with complete obedience and servility. Thaddeus was not above raising his voice or even his hand on his grown children. It was not unheard-of for Donnie and Caitlin to appear in public with red marks on their cheeks, marks they did not even consider necessary to conceal. All parents slap their children. It's only one of the expressions of love. One must be a hopeless idiot or an ungrateful bastard to think otherwise. Enduring occasional scolding from their father was a small price to pay for comfort and security. In their eyes it was a perfectly healthy, natural discourse between family members. Father O'Malley, the parish priest, referred to this cheerful, thankful parasitism as "filial piety". To declare independence from one's parents was to openly proclaim one's superiority. Did Hugh think himself so far above the rest of the Malones, since he did not wish to remain indebted to them?

Did he truly believe that by securing some posh situation in Belfast, he could ransom himself from his father and buy his freedom?

The longer Donnie pondered Hugh's words, the more confused he grew, and that confusion only fueled his anger. That scrawny, sneezing, wheezing, droopy-nosed weakling, who had nothing to shoe for himself except for some glossy piece of paper called diploma, that curly-haired, mud-colored Jew look-alike dared to insult him, Don Joseph McCluskey, his sacred clan and the entire tradition that had existed for centuries! Had it not been for Mrs. Malone and the remnants of her heavenly cherry pie, Donnie would have punched Hugh in the face right there. Yes, that crooked nose was begging to be smashed!

Suddenly, Donnie stretched his neck out and sniffed the air.

"What's that?" he asked, instantly forgetting about his desire to avenge his family's honor. "Smells like burnin' leather…"

Hugh looked into the furnace and jumped up from his chair, dropping his notebook on the floor.

"Dylan!" he shouted, throwing his arms up in disbelief. "I knew you've gone mad. Those were your new shoes. You wore them once for the graduation banquet!"

"And the tie too," Dylan, added proudly. "That's what they made us wear in college, Don. Our professors demanded that we look civil. MacNeill, the one who taught Irish history, was the worst. He wouldn't let you inside his lecture hall without a vest, and he wouldn't greet you on the street if you didn't wear a bowler hat. But I'm home now. Nobody gives me orders save for Dadaí."

"Well-done, chieftain," Hugh muttered aside, mimicking his father. "It's a shame Dadaí wasn't here to see this. I can only imagine how proud he'd be."

The heat from the campfire enhanced the smell of hay in the night air. About thirty people sat in a tight circle in the yard behind Colin O'Nevin's house. Those gatherings took place at least every other day. That heart-mending custom gave the inhabitants of the Tulsk village a chance to send all the secular troubles to hell and pass a few pitchers of ale around the circle.

The days were filled with temptations to gain new enemies. It could be Jim Hagerty's overly adventurous pig running into the neighbor's kitchen garden. Or, it could be the crazy Ben McKeever smashing somebody's window with a bottle. By God, was it possible to count all the unpleasant casualties? Those few hours spent together sufficed to glue together the feeble sense of unity in people. Old and young would forget their age, because the songs they sang in one howling voice were ageless.

The sounds produced by Dylan Flynn's fiddle sealed most of the cracks in one's heart, chasing out the resentment. Without words that pride would never let them say out loud, the villagers pressed each other's hands. Parting, they were friends, at least until another day.

That evening during the campfire Dylan Malone slipped a ring on Caitlin's finger and planted an unskilled but generous kiss on her lips. She was the only girl he had ever kissed, though he had had his share of opportunities with the ladies in Dublin. Fortunately, his bride was as inexperienced and indiscriminating as he.

Caitlin had a daunting task before her—to outbreed her big brother Donnie, who already had three children. She promised herself that she would not fall behind him. Aside from the Church's praise of large families, it was the only expression of sibling rivalry available to her and Donnie, since neither one of them had any other passions or abilities. Dylan Malone made for a perfect helpmate in Caitlin's quest for parental attention. For the past five years, Thaddeus McCluskey and his wife had been preoccupied with Donnie's offspring: baptisms for the three surviving children, and the funerals for the two that died shortly after birth. Now it was Caitlin's turn to be the queen of the hive. Judging from the ferocity of her hunger and by the rapid expansion of her waist, Caitlin concluded that she was carrying more than one baby. At least, that is what she wished to believe. Oh, wouldn't that be a fist to the chin for Donnie! The first set of twins in the McCluskey clan. Her Dadaí had already splurged on a cottage with Mr. Malone. It was tolerable for starters, although, Caitlin would have preferred something taller and more spacious. Next, she would convince her parents to build a barn, too, or maybe buy a new buggy, so she and Dylan could ride out to Athlone.

They were sitting aside from everyone else, in that corner of the yard that the campfire did not illuminate so brightly. Caitlin was reluctant to display herself on people, afraid that her condition might become a new subject for gossips, and never left the house without a huge woolen shawl.

"I'll look like hell in a weddin' dress, all because you just couldn't wait," she reproached Dylan jokingly.

"To me you'll be the loveliest, always, should you even grow horns," Dylan answered, quite earnestly.

"Let's pray it never happens!" She laughed and tightened her arms around his neck. "I'm so relieved you won't be returnin' to Dublin."

"Four years of college is more than 'nough for me. Now I must quickly rid it everythin' needless that I learned there, before my wretched head cracks. But Hugh, our darlin' mad scholar, already misses his teachers."

"Where is your brother?" Caitlin asked, straightening out. "I haven't seen much of him as of late. Why is he hidin'? I'll tell you a secret. Alison O'Mara has been lovesick for him since last summer. She keeps sayin' how wished that Hugh Malone would look her way at last."

"Poor Alison…" Dylan smirked.

"Why is she poor? They'd make a grand pair. Homely ones always find refuge in one another."

"It's not that simple, love."

"Surely, it's that simple!"

"It may be too late for Alison. My baby brother has already found refuge in someone else."

Caitlin chuckled, assuming that Dylan was joking.

"Now, who on earth would have Hugh?"

"It isn't my right to tell."

"Oh, you can tell me!" Caitlin exclaimed, enraged by Dylan's last declaration. "I'm carrying your bastard under my heart, confined to my house all day, ashamed to go to church. Don't I deserve to hear a bit of family gossip?"

What could Dylan possibly say to counter that argument? He knew that Caitlin was in the right. The girl had already mastered the art of strategic reproach and guilt.

"So be it," Dylan whispered, surrendering. "But keep in mind, it is still a secret. I haven't even told Donnie yet. Hugh doesn't look at any of the girls 'round here 'cause he's already married, to an English girl, a professor's daughter."

Caitlin gasped and crossed herself.

"Christ, have mercy!"

"My exact words."

"What became of that wench who lived on Frankfurt Avenue?"

"Isabel McCormack?"

"Yes. Wasn't her stepfather some Polish prince?"

"A count! Markey… Hell, I still cannot pronounce his bloody family name. Nothin' came of it! Hugh sang for her. She fed him caviar. They kissed and parted ways. In the end, he married an Englishwoman."

"Well," Caitlin continued, growing more agitated, "didn't you try to stop him?"

"What on earth could I do? When did my brother listen to me or anyone else for that matter? That English witch cast a spell on him."

"What's her name?"

"Edith Ashley."

"She ought to apologize for her name alone." Pregnancy made Caitlin merciless and all the more patriotic.

"Oh, I hated her brother," Dylan continued. "Bein' a professor's son and all, he acted like a bastard with no fear of punishment. He kept callin' me Potato Prince, until one day I thrashed him so hard that he forgot his own name. Remember the time they almost expelled me? But his sister isn't altogether terrible. She's homely, no doubt, and she's older than him by a few years. But she earns good money, from what I hear. Damn good money."

"Doin' what?"

"Playin' piano."

The very concept of a woman earning damn good money struck Caitlin as something out of the realm of fantasy. The fact that the allegedly lucrative job did not involve baking or sewing made it all the more mysterious. A piano? Caitlin could not recall ever seeing one. In the eighteen years of her life, she had not seen a musical instrument larger than a squeezebox. Just like her big brother, Caitlin was angered by the things she did not understand.

Suddenly, the abstract Englishwoman turned into a tangible enemy.

"How much they pay her?" she asked without concealing her jealousy.

"I don't know, love," Dylan replied. "Hugh won't tell me. I bet it's more than they do for your sewin'. But she's a homely one, and money can't be buyin' beauty," he added hastily, seeing that his bride was beginning to fume.

Jealous Caitlin always welcomed an opportunity to discuss the ugliness of another woman, especially if she was English.

"Tell me then, what's her ugliest feature?"

"Oh, I wouldn't know where to begin," Dylan muttered, uneasy about the direction that the conversation was taking.

Truth be told, his new sister-in-law was far from ugly. As a matter of fact, she was quite beautiful, within the frame of her Anglo-Saxon breed, of course. Still, Dylan needed to invent a convincing lie about her physical flaws to appease his bride.

"You know, poor Hugh's near-sighted," he said at last. "Even with his glasses, he can't always tell a pretty woman from an ugly one. Lucky for Edith! She got herself a blind husband! All they do is talk. Best of all, her father found Hugh a position in Belfast, tutorin' some Englishman's son."

Having gotten her hunger for scandal satiated, Caitlin warmed up once again and clung to Dylan as tightly as her swelling belly allowed.

"But what 'bout your father?" she asked. "He'll raise hell when he finds out."

Dylan cringed and shook his head, as if forcing a mouthful of bitter medicine down his throat.

"Caitlin, my love, it won't be a pretty sight, upon my soul. God knows, I don't want to be there when it happens. Or rather, I ought to be there, if only to shield my reckless baby brother from Dadaí."

In the twenty years of their siblinghood, Dylan had never needed to shield Hugh from their father, even though he had rescued him countless times from the neighborhood boys. Brendan had never raised his hand on his youngest son, although he had spouted some rather impressive threats. Caitlin had heard some of those threats.

"And why does your father keep sayin' that he'll shoot Hugh?" she asked Dylan suddenly. "What sort of an ill joke is that?"

"Oh, that's nothin', just a prophecy of some mad old gypsy. I never told you how it happened, did I? So listen. It's quite a story."

***

Dylan remembered that day quite clearly, even though he was no older than five at the time. He remembered the spring fair in Athlone, the smothering, humid sunshine, the smell of tobacco and grass trodden into the ground. He even remembered the embroidery on his mother's new blouse and the cornflowers woven into her braided hair.

Brendan was hoping to purchase another rifle. That was the main goal of his trip to the fair. Even though the law prohibited the sale of weapons in that place, he knew exactly where to go. He knew the small plain tent and its owner, who kept firearms under the counter.

Máirín, in her turn, was sighing over a corral necklace, even though she knew she was not going to take it home, as her husband did not believe that a married woman, a mother of two boys, needed such adornments.

Suddenly, a gray-haired hag from the fortune-teller's booth beckoned her.

"Come closer, dearie."

That strange voice, neither young nor old, neither male nor female, seemed to be coming from the fortune-teller's eyes and not her mouth. Her colorless lips were barely moving. Yet Máirín and her two children heard the call distinctly.

The hag belonged to the tribe of nomads known as the Travelers, who referred to themselves as *Pavees*. She had not come to the fair alone. Her fellow-tribesmen had brought purebred greyhound pups and young stallions.

Máirín patted her flat purse sorrowfully, letting the fortune-teller know that it was empty, but the old woman shook her ragged locks and came out of the booth towards her.

"I don't want your money, dearie. There's something you must know about your husband. He's a cursed man."

Brendan, who until then had been bargaining with the rifle peddler, overheard the gypsy's words and turned around.

"Get the hell away from my wife!"

The old woman ignored the threat and kept on muttering to Máirín, jerking her by the embroidered sleeve.

"Hear me out, dearie, for your sons' sake. It's not too late to save them yet. Take them and run from that man, or he'll be the end of them and you, too."

This time Brendan, who had never been too fond of the Travelers, seized her by the arm, dark and dry, like a dead tree branch.

"What're you mumblin'? It's your filthy tribe that's cursed. I'll break your bloody arm off!"

The fortune-teller pulled away with a hiss. Her sparse gray hair rose at the roots.

"Swear all you want! Call to your God! He won't help you. Nor will help your eldest son when he bleeds before your eyes. And your youngest son, mark my word, will turn against you. You'll kill him with your own hands, with that very rifle you bought. I saw the future in your wife's eyes. They're full of tears yet to spill. She'll die a wretched woman if she stays with you."

***

"So goes the prophecy," Dylan concluded his story. "I recall bein' so frightened that day, not so much by the fortune-teller's words as by her looks. One ugly hag she was. Mamaí even began to cry. I thought that Dadaí would kill the old witch for sure, but she slipped away just in time."

Caitlin dropped her chin to her chest and let out a sigh the purpose of which was to ravish Dylan with guilt.

"What's the matter with you now?" he asked.

"Now, why did you tell me that story?"

"Well, because you asked me, love!" Dylan replied light-heartedly.

"That was before I knew the story would mention you bleeding to death. You should've known not to worry me so, not whilst I'm with child. Now, thanks to you I won't sleep at night."

"Oh, don't you start frettin' now!" Dylan laughed and bounced Caitlin on his knee. "What's there to fear? Who believes those pagans anyway? They'll tell you anythin'. Dadaí doesn't believe it either. That's why he jokes 'bout it all the time. Listen, you stay here for a minute, and I'll run home to fetch Hugh. He's goin' to Belfast soon, and we won't even hear him sing 'The Island of Sorrow'. Nobody can sing it like him."

Dylan headed towards his house, but half way he ran into his father.

"Don't I have a surprise for you," Brendan said. "Hugh already knows. Guess where I'm takin' you both first thin' tomorrow mornin'? I've been promisin' you that trip for long..."

"Carrick?" Dylan asked, beaming. "Carrick, at last?"

Brendan nodded.

"Tomorrow wi' the sunrise we're headin' there. At last, you'll meet my friends. Now there're your friends, too. What men they are! Many think them plain mad. But if the Irish Republic ever comes around, they'll be the only ones to thank for it."

***

Dylan had spent the rest of the evening under the effect of his father's words. Every once in a while he would turn his eyes to Hugh, wondering if his brother was feeling the same elation, but there was no sign of euphoria upon Hugh's face, even when he stood up in the middle of the circle and performed the tragic ballad written to the lyrics of Thomas Moore:

Though he lived for his love, it's for his country he died.
They were all that to life had entwined him
The tears of his country may never be dried,
Nor long will his love stay behind him.
So make her the grave where the sun goes to rest,
And think of the glorious tomorrow.
Make shine on her sleep like a smile from the West,
On her own lovely Island of Sorrow...

Hugh's performance was not completely deprived of passion, but that passion was anything but patriotic. His voice quivered at the word "love" but not "country". His sympathy towards Sarah's Curran for losing her fiancé clearly overshadowed than the one towards Ireland for losing a soldier. Hugh stared into the heart of the campfire where the crimson tongues burnt the brightest, shaping into figures. As soon as people started applauding, he bowed hastily and hid in the back rows of the circle.

Having assured that the public attention shifted onto the O'Nevin brothers, he took a tobacco box from his pocket. On the back of the silver lid there was a woman's portrait. For a few minutes Hugh looked at the thin face in the aura of light hair, and then brought it to his lips.

"What're you kissin' there?" Brendan asked him suspiciously.

Hugh did not realize that his father was nearby, smoking his pipe quietly.

"Nothing, Dadaí. I was just sniffing tobacco."

"Listen to him – sniffin' tobacco! You don't even smoke. You can't stand the very smell. Your precious nose will bleed. Here's my advice, don't bother lyin' if you're no good at it. And where did you get that box? It looks very much like silver. You worry me, lad, at times. See that you do nothin' foolish."

"I shall try not to, Dadaí," Hugh promised, hiding the box in his pocket.

***

Having returned home that evening, Hugh found his mother in a particularly sentimental disposition. Máirín started suddenly recalling how in the summers long past her little lads would sleep under the stars. She brought two mattresses from the house, threw them on the grass and sat between them with a jug of cider in her hands. The boys, moved by their mother's ability to remember such endearing trifles, eagerly accepted her proposal to revisit childhood and sprawled out on the mattresses. In that manner they spent about half an hour thus, listening to fairy-tales and sipping half-fermented apple juice.

That idyll did not last long. Brendan barged in and interrupted the scene.

"How damned sweet!" he smirked. "Well, woman, I guess I'll give you another minute to bid your darlin' pups good-night."

"One minute?" Máirín asked. "Why only one?"

"Well, did you intend on sittin' here all night? You'll keep them awake with your old wives' tales, and they need to rest. Tomorrow they're commin' with me to Carrick-on-Shannon. I haven't seen my comrades in six months, and I can't go any longer."

Máirín flushed and turned her shoulders out. She could count the times she dared to challenge her husband.

"And I haven't seen my sons in year! And you're already takin' them away on another wild exploit! Isn't it bad enough that I worry myself to death each time you go there? What do you do with those idiot mates of yours besides playin' with dynamite? One day, they'll bring you home with your legs blown off. That will serve you right. At least leave my children out of your pranks!"

"'Nough of that, woman!" Brendan howled imploringly rather than menacingly. "I've a mighty headache now. See what you've done to me?"

"And I endure heartache every day. I suppose that doesn't count. I burn my fingers on the hot stove and slice them with a sickle, but none of those injuries hurt. No, mothers feel no pain, save for that of their children."

"Very well, then. All that talk of pain! You've asked for it."

Brendan made a rapid step towards his wife, caught her by the wrist and bent her index finger backwards. This application of force was not to intimidate but rather to pacify, and it worked beautifully this time, just as it had worked hundreds of times before.

"I'm not hurtin' you, silly woman," Brendan spoke in a reconciliatory tone. "See? I'm not the one pullin' you fingers 'part. You're doin' it to yourself. Whose fault is it that you're hurtin' now?"

Máirín let out a few gasps and bowed her head. When she raised it again, streams of tears were gushing down her cheeks.

"Lads, you saw it with your own eyes," Brendan addressed his sons. "Did I hurt your Mamaí?"

The boys remained silent after their custom. Sadly, it was not the first time they were witnessing such a scene. They already knew how it would all resolve.

"I just asked you, did I hurt your Mamaí?" he repeated the question, raising his voice slightly. "Or did she bring it 'pon herself?"

"Mamaí brought it 'pon herself," Dylan replied energetically, as it was the only way to make the father take pity on the mother and release her.

"You hear that, silly woman?" Brendan asked, bringing his face closer to his wife's. "Your own children agree with me. You've got no business stirrin' such trouble."

He kissed her gently on the temple, gave her middle finger one last reminder jerk and let go of it. Wavering, Máirín threw one last entreating glance at Hugh.

"Will at least you stay?" she asked him in a dying voice, oblivious to the presence of her husband and eldest son. "You're a reasonable boy. You know how much your Mamaí worries."

"I already promised Dadaí that I would go," Hugh replied. "Don't cry, Mamaí. There will be no playing with dynamite this time. We'll save the fireworks for the harvest season. It is only to meet a few friends. We'll return with our legs and other parts intact, I assure you."

"There, you've heard your pet, woman," Brendan concluded. "All shall be well. Now, quit whinin' and go inside."

Máirín covered her face and disappeared inside the house where she immediately fell on her knees before the statue of the Virgin and started praying for her husband to regain his wits. Brendan realized that there was no use in him trying his luck in the marital bed that night, so he sprawled on the grass between his sons.

"Now, march yourselves to sleep," he commanded. "And you better not snore."

Naturally, Brendan was the first one to begin snoring, contrary to his own command. Both sons remained awake. Dylan raised himself on the elbow and began whispered to Hugh in broken Gaelic, as a gratuitous precaution, lest their father should catch the gist of their conversation through his slumber.

"Are you asleep?"

"Not a chance."

"Me neither. Listen, tonight I almost spilled your secret to Dadaí. You know I'd never give you away, not even under torture. Burn me, scourge me, break my bones, and I won't make a sound. I don't feel my own pain. But tonight Dadaí poured me some whiskey, lit a pipe, winked and asked:,'Talk to me, chieftain. What sort of mischief did you cause in the capitol?' I could tell he mostly wanted to hear 'bout your adventures. Everyone knows what I've been doin', thrashin' Trinity lads and skippin' Latin. But my sweet, baby brother pulled somethin' truly bold. He took it 'pon himself to reconcile two nations that have been warrin' for quite a few years. Bloody diplomat!"

"Oh, stop it. Don't exaggerate. I just fell in love, that's all."

"You didn't *just* fall in love. You fell in love out of spite. Clearly, our women aren't good enough for you. You must prove to the world that you're better than us. Ah, to hell with that. And even if you did just fall for that haughty witch, what then, eh? Maybe we should all just drop our duties and follow our hearts! That's somethin' a common peasant can do. You're a Fenian's son. Sure, you can fancy anyone you please, but you marry your own kind. You do what Dadaí says, for the good of the country."

"Ah, here we go again, the good of the country. A country where the potato rots, bacon grows stale and patriotic sentiments ferment like moonshine—"

"Kill the poet. When do you intend on breakin' the news to Dadaí?"

"When the time is right," Hugh replied, staring at the starless sky.

"Dadaí senses that somethin' is amiss. He tried to point out a few unmarried girls, but you didn't even look their way. You can't deceive him for long. I'm tellin' you, Dadaí already knows. He just doesn't believe it yet. The truth hasn't sunk in. And when it does, he'll shoot you, mark my word. He'll probably shoot me, too, for havin' allowed it to happen. He had ordered me to watch you closely."

"Ah, he won't shoot either one of us. Just think of how stupid he'll look arriving at the camp alone. What will he tell his mates? Everything shall be well."

"Are you certain of it?"

"Of course, I'm not certain, you fool. I am not certain of anything except that I cannot spend another summer here. I shall go to the river just to humor Dadaí, but afterwards... Think of me fondly."

"So, this is where the road splits?"

"The road had split years ago. I promise to write."

Roused by their hissing, Brendan stopped snoring and stirred.

"What are you mumblin'?" he asked, his eyes still closed.

"Nothin', Dadaí," Dylan replied in English, his voice atremble. "We were just sayin' our nighttime prayers in Gaelic."

"Well, keep 'em short. We've got a long and crooked road lyin' ahead of us."

The trip was long indeed, though not entirely unpleasant. At the turn of the century the entire Eastern Connaught, the midlands removed from the salty waters and nourished instead by the river Shannon, was one of those fortunate places still innocent of industrial or even agrarian horrors.

Brendan, following a romantic whim, decided to travel by horse across the nearest bridge. A boat ride to Carrick-on-Shannon was too easy, simply not heroic enough. Having seized an early start, by sunrise, the three men had already left the myriad patches of potato fields behind and entered the kingdom of moist woods.

Happy to break free from his village life and looking forward to an entire week at Carrick-on-Shannon, Brendan lit his pipe. He could not wait to flaunt his sons before his comrades.

"June's the best month of the year," he spoke between puffs of smoke. "The summer's still young, and the hottest days still ahead. I married your Mamaí in June, and in January of next year Dylan was born." Brendan released the reigns for an instant, flung his arms open and arched his back. "Our weddin' night was dismal. Your Mamaí was weak and nauseous all the while, with throbbin' breasts I couldn't touch and red teary eyes that gazed 'pon me with hatred. Half the night I listened to her grievances. By four in the mornin', I was ready to flee from the marriage bed and seek refuge in the hay barn, the same hay barn where we had tumbled two months earlier. 'Twas made clear I wasn't goin' to get any relief until after the child's birth. For how eager she was the first time I took her, she behaved mighty prickly on the weddin' night. Ah, such is the price a young groom pays for bein' hasty. Why am I sharin' this with you? Don't believe Father O'Malley or anyone else who tells you that the Irish had more decency in the old days. Are you listenin', Dylan?"

"Yes, Dadaí..."

"If Father O'Malley gives you grief, don't take it to heart. Just nod and look thoroughly ashamed, but don't let yourself feel any shame deep underneath. Twenty years ago, our men were just as impatient and our women just as immodest. We're a lusty breed! That's one way to ensure survival."

Brendan laughed and spurred his horse. Dylan mimicked him, leaving his younger brother behind. Hugh was secretly praying that his horse would break its leg, so he could turn around and walk home. He had not sat in the saddle in over a year, and his body had forgotten the joys of being jostled back and forth. After just an hour of riding down the steep rocky paths that his father found so pleasing to the eye, Hugh was in mild agony. His entire back was aching, as if he had been caned, and he could not feel his legs below the knee. He sneezed and saw droplets of blood on the palm of his hand. If only the horse would stumble. Wouldn't that be a blessing! Hugh would not even mind getting a little bruised, if it would save him from the trip to Carrick. He could not bear to hear any more hay barn stories involving his poor mother, whose fingers got wrought before his very eyes just the night before.

"Hey now, don't fall asleep!" Brendan shouted at Hugh, glancing over his shoulder. "Spur the bloody horse! A fine stallion he is, one of the fastest and the sturdiest ones from the stable. I wouldn't let the lads at Carrick see my sons ridin' sickly mares."

Hugh kicked his horse's side, hoping it would get startled, charge ahead and throw him off, but the stallion was too well-trained. It did not even twitch from the blow of the rider's boot.

"I wonder what news the lads got for me," Brendan continued when both of his sons were riding by his side once again. "I haven't seen them in six months. I bet they've cooked up a new risin' by now. Let's hope it won't be like the one in '67. By the way, did they even teach you that in college? I bet they omitted the best parts. Do you even know how it all started?"

Dylan and Hugh knew exactly how it started and how it ended, for they had heard the same story a hundred times, with slight variations. Still, they knew not to interrupt their father, because the story happened to be his heart's ballad of which he never grew tired. And, since Brendan was too young to have witnessed most of what had happened in that turbulent segment of time between the Crimean War of 1850s and the Land Wars of the 1880s, he could tell only what he heard from others. Dylan and Hugh could recite the history of the IRB even in their sleep.

The Irish Republican Brotherhood, that secret, oath-bound society of starving urban intellectuals, small landowners and others who had reasons for discontentment with the system, was a dream-child of James Stephens, an ambitious Kilkenian, in the year of Our Lord 1858. The Fenian spirit had spread quietly and swiftly, like an underground river, reaching as far to the west as North America. Those immigrants that had fled Ireland during the Great Famine eagerly replied to Stephens' appeal and started sending funds to their former motherland in support of the Brotherhood. In less than a decade, the number of the IRB members had grown to eighty thousand, all to Stephens' jubilant amazement.

"Mind you, most of the early Fenians were such in name alone, all through the 1860s," Brendan spoke disparagingly of his predecessors. "Very few bore arms, and even they didn't know how to use them. I once had the famous photo of the 'Cuba Five' where John Devoy and four of his mates are sittin' in two straight rows, lookin' like Angels of Enlight'ment, all in dark suits, their hair combed back smoothly. One mustn't be deceived by that picture. Most of the Fenians didn't measure up to that lofty ideal, in looks or in spirit. God knows, the Brotherhood didn't lack willin' hearts. They were short of calculatin' minds. Stephens said so himself. Not that it kept him from startin' a risin'! Oh, he had his heart set on seein' the first great battle. And sure enough, it happened! In March of 1867 a few thousand Fenians appeared in Dublin, Cork, Tipperary and Limerick. You should've seen the poor devils rushin' like a herd of mad horses onto a wall of spears. It did not take long to suppress them, just the local police and a blizzard. A few skirmishes and a few dead Englishmen, such was the long-awaited glory. In the civilians' eyes, the Fenians didn't deserve much sympathy until the day the three of them were executed in Manchester. They became known as—"

"The Manchester Martyrs!" Dylan and Hugh howled in unison.

"That's right," Brendan confirmed solemnly and raised a trembling fist. "And just before his death on the gallows, each one of them shouted—"

"God save Ireland!"

The father and the sons bowed their heads and took a few seconds of silence, as it was customary after citing those words.

"And then T.D. Sullivan composed a song," Hugh added with feigned enthusiasm, grateful that his father, who was riding ahead, could not see him roll his eyes.

"And the song became the unofficial national anthem!" Dylan concluded triumphantly. "And I sang it on St. Patrick's Day, under the balcony of Countess Markiewicz, the Godmother of the Irish youth!"

Around noon Brendan decided to make a halt a few miles from Elphin town. The horses were tired and thirsty, and the boys were hungry. Unfortunately, he had not brought any food with him except for a small loaf of stale soda bread and a jug of ale. Apparently, he expected that a lush feast would be waiting for them at the camp.

While the horses were drinking from the river, and the boys were picking up bread crumbs from their trousers, the proud father continued the history lesson.

"After the failed rebellion of 1867, the remainin' Fenians spent a few decades lickin' their wounds. They did away with the fancy hierarchy. No more colonels, sergeants or captains. No more titles of any sort. The Fenians clustered together to form tiny circles led by chieftains, just like in the times of Finn McCumhail. Forty years ago, in the whole of Ireland there were about fifteen circles. The one I belong to is among the oldest ones. That clearin' on the west bank of Shannon makes for a perfect meetin' place. Most of the lads who frequent that came are from Strokestown and Frenchpark. Some come all the way from Athlone. At night they make bonfires and bake small fowl and potatoes. Every now and then you'll hear tin whistle through the sleepy woods. There are many fine musicians among them. They all look like brothers, too. You'd swear they all leaped out of the same womb."

"Or out of the same edition of *Punch* magazine," Hugh remarked venomously.

Brendan cleared his throat and gave his youngest a stare that was both quizzical and menacing. He had seen enough copies of *Punch* to understand Hugh's hint. The illustrators of the magazine took pleasure in portraying the Irish as kettle-headed, apes with crooked legs, square jaws and poorly groomed sideburns.

"Were you tryin' to say somethin', son?" Brendan asked.

"When people spend too much time together, eating the same food, playing the same music and defending the same ideals, they start looking alike. It is a scientific fact. How do you think various species and breeds emerge in the animal kingdom? It's rudimentary Darwinism."

Hugh shrugged and forced the last piece of dry soda bread down his throat.

"Forgive me," Dylan mumbled. "I've drunk the last of your ale. Don't start chokin' now, baby brother. Or else your nose shall bleed."

"Oh yes, bleed it shall," Brendan said, his eyes on Hugh, "once I break it."

Feeling the temperature rising, Dylan quickly moved in between his father and his younger brother.

"Dadaí, tell us how the Fenians fell into disgrace with the Catholic Church," he begged. "Were they not on the same side? Were they not both enemies of the Protestant England? You must explain it to me, Dadaí. I don't want to look foolish before your mates."

"Oh, I can explain it for you," Hugh replied imperturbably and assumed a more militant pose. "To quote a certain bishop from Kerry: 'When we look down into the fathomless depth of this infamy of the heads of the Fenian conspiracy, we must acknowledge that eternity is not long enough, nor hell hot enough to punish such miscreants.'"

Having grown accustomed to quoting philosophers during presentations, Hugh articulated out the bishop's remark effortlessly on one breath.

"You see, Rome does not endorse any conspiracy except for its own," he continued. "For the sake of fairness, one could not judge the bishop too harshly. He was merely performing his catechism-dictated duty, which is to intimidate. What terrible sins had the Fenians committed after all? A few railroads blown up? Bah! There was no more brutality in their deeds than in the Crusades. Sometimes, having a common enemy is not enough to unite two entities. Does that answer your question, big brother?"

Even though Hugh was addressing Dylan, his gaze remained on Brendan. The father and his son became engaged in a staring competition. They could not put their fists to use, so they had to rely on words and stares.

"Dadaí, I hear there's a Fenian shrine nearby," Dylan said in a trembling voice. He seized his father by the shoulders in hopes that Brendan would finally stop scourging Hugh with his eyes. "Since the bishop wouldn't give the Fenians his blessing, they built a chapel of their own. They go there to pray to St. Lawrence O'Toole, their patron saint. Can you take us there?"

"Ah, I hear it's but an abandoned old hut," Hugh said, flicking his wrist spitefully. "They just hung some crosses and icons on the walls. There's more cobweb than religious art. It is nothing spectacular, truly. However, if you are dying to hear the O'Toole litany, I'll be happy to recite it for you."

"Please do," Brendan requested coldly and stuffed his hands in the pockets of his trousers, mainly to keep them from gripping his youngest by the throat. "Dylan and I would like to hear it."

Hugh rose to his feet, flexed his back and chanted:

Call to thine aid, O most liberty-loving O'Toole,
Whose Christian auxiliaries of power and glory –
The soul-inspiring cannon, the meek and faithful musket,
The pious rifle, and the conscience-examining pike,
Which tempered by a martyr's faith,
A Fenian hope, and a rebel's charity,
Will triumph over the devil,
And restore to us our own in our land for ever.

Now, who would dare to deny that this prayer had the power to convert the most stubborn cynics into romantics? The hymn blew over the deserted banks of the Shannon, skimming the surface of the water. The mockery in Hugh's melodic baritone could not elude his father.

"Well done, bard!" Brendan praised him. "You forgot to say 'Amen' in the end. Unless, of course, you meant to leave that word out."

He certainly could not fault Hugh for lack of knowledge of the Fenian lore. If only he could convince his son to embrace it!

The first thing the three travelers saw when they rode into the Fenian camp outside Carrick-on-Shannon was a handful of middle-aged men sitting on the river's bank, staring into the weedy waters, rocking from side to side, bumping shoulders, smoking pipes and swapping anecdotes.

"Hey, Mahoney?"

"What is it, Costello?"

"I say, 'tis pity that Nevin and Garvin aren't here."

"What's become of them?"

"Can't you recall? They both perished in South Africa, in Transvaal. I saw it happen, for I was there myself."

"So? That was ages ago, and so far away. What the deuce ye recall 'em for?"

"How should I know? They were good men."

"So let 'em rest in peace, Costello."

"In that heathen negro land, Mahoney? How can they rest in peace there? I told them not to join the British army."

***

That year there was a multitude of young men at the camp. It was a sorely needed infusion of fresh blood. By 1900 the Fenian leaders were growing disheartened, as there were no new recruits joining their ranks. Had the recurring defeats of the previous century chilled the hearts of the younger generation?

The Republican renaissance had begun with the homecoming of Tom Clarke, a veteran Fenian, who had spent fifteen years in British jails for his attempt to blow up London Bridge. His imprisonment had been followed by a seven-year year exile in America. When he returned to Ireland in 1907 with his beautiful and much younger wife, a wave of agitation ran through the sleepy Fenian ranks. Having settled in Dublin with his new family, Clarke established a tobacco shop and immediately dove into his Fenian cause, more daring and impassioned than he was twenty-five years earlier. Imprisonment and exile had not shattered his spirits or even his health. Clarke looked as if he had spent two decades in a health resort, playing golf and feasting on fruit. There was not a hint of bitterness or disillusionment in his eyes. His shop became a pilgrimage destination for the capitol's young nationalists. They trickled in only to shake the hand of their Fenian father-figure and to listen to his tales.

Then, in late summer of 1909 Constance Markiewicz, the older, the prettier and the more radical one of the infamous Gore-Booth sisters, the one who had married the dashing Polish nobleman, helped found *Na Fianna Eireann*, a youth movement akin to that of boy-scouts, which became the salvation for the withering Brotherhood. The inaugural meeting took place in a dingy hall, but later, the Countess rented a house that became the headquarters for the organization and an oasis for idealistic children, where they could play with loaded rifles, practice target shooting and learn the rudiments of first medical aid without anyone threatening them with eternal damnation. The aging Fenians of O'Mahoney's era included the Countess' name into each prayer, along with those of Denis McCullough, Bulmer Hobson and Helena Molony, a ravishing auburn-haired suffragette.

***

Because of some festivity taking place in Carrick that day, the boys, already tipsy, gathered in circles and danced to the counterfeit melodies of fiddles and tin whistles. Some tossed cards or rolled dice right on the grass, while the observers of the game marked every loss with a vigorous howl. Their stories seemed more animated and less nostalgic than the ones of their fathers.

"Hey, Callaghan, won't you tell us how you met the witch?"

"'Twasn't me, you lout, but Gallagher, who's no longer with us. He offended some wench who happened to be a witch. She kept sendin' him frightful dreams, until he shot himself through the head. But I've got a better story yet. Know why nobody's livin' in that hut at the end of the village? That's cause the chimney keeps growlin' at night, like a tiny babe cryin'. There was a hussy, they say, who birthed a bastard. She feared shame, so she stuck the wretched babe in the chimney and lit the stove. It died there of all the smoke and fire. And since it died without a proper baptism, its soul didn't go to God but remained in the chimney. So, it keeps lamentin' and cursin' its mother, night after night."

The listeners started gasping with at once horror and delight. Only Dan Flannegan, who resented Ed Callaghan's ability to draw everyone's attention to himself, shrugged his shoulder with feigned bore. "I know a better story about one man's soul trapped inside a whiskey bottle."

"Ah, don't mention a whiskey bottle, unless you intend on breakin' one open!"

It took no more than a few seconds for some foolish quarrel to turn into a fist fight. Old scabs would begin bleeding again, and loose teeth would become a little looser. Then suddenly, driven by fraternal tenderness, the adversaries would laugh and fall into each other's arms.

"Ian, forgive me!"

"No, Brian, you forgive me! I shouldn't have said that, really. God knows, if you started callin' me Mamaí names, I'd kill you, that's for sure."

***

Not quite ready for another organized rebellion, the Fenians did not waste time and rebelled at least against the British fashion. It was the first step to asserting their independence from the British aesthetics. By the early 1900's, those tight short breeches and bulky shoes depicted on the early cartoons became rare. Only the old town officials would be seen wearing those. The younger Fenians, pursuing a manlier look preferred looser trousers tucked inside riding boots. On each shirt the top buttons on the shirts were missing, leaving the collars unfastening wide, revealing necks and chests with large Celtic crosses on plain threads. All boys had their sleeves rolled up, a subtle reminder that they were always ready to perform butchers' job. Still, the most astonishing, the most dazzling of all was the unifying expression upon their fresh, healthy faces, the one of fanatical bliss.

Watching them, Hugh felt a chill between his ribs. His horror doubled when he saw how quickly the atmosphere absorbed into his own brother's skin. Dylan's eyes turned glassy like they would when he fell ill with high fever. He seized his father's arm.

"Well, son, you like it here?" Brendan asked, smiling approvingly.

Dylan mumbled something incoherent.

"I knew you'd love this place. Go no further in your search for Heaven. And you, Hugh? Why're you sittin' so quiet? Come, look 'round!"

"I'm looking," Hugh replied with involuntary tremor in his voice. "I'm looking."

They left the horses in the stable and proceeded along a narrow path covered with tiny rocks and dry pine needles. Suddenly, all three trembled. Through the mixture of voices and counterfeit fiddle tunes, they heard a woman's laughter.

Beneath an old poplar, surrounded by a dozen young Fenians, stood a girl around twenty, in a gray dress with loose transparent sleeves and a garland of crimson poppy flowers on her head. Her black hair braided with that lovely deliberate negligence only half way. Some stout youngster about her age sat at her feet, every now and then pulling her skirt, while she continued to ignore him. Another boy, his arm around her waist, kept whispering in her ear, apparently something very amusing and wicked, judging by the wild expression of her slanted gray eyes. Each time she laughed he kissed her cheek and buried his glistening face on her shoulder. Still, one could see that her acceptance of his puppyish caresses held no promises.

Hugh instantly recognized the girl to be the Polish Count's stepdaughter, his guardian deity who tutored him in Latin, helped him deconstruct the Enlightenment philosophers, read and critiqued his epic poems that nobody else would read, and who fed him salmon and cucumber sandwiches when he had no money to buy bread and butter. Hugh recalled the glorious April evening at the villa on Frankfurt Avenue, the humid living room stuffed with giddy, drunken Poles, the smell of musk and spilled sherry and his own voice singing the "Green Sleeves". Two years had passed since then. His adolescent flame for Isabel had since subsided, but the admiration remained, for Hugh never deleted any pleasant moment from his memory. On more than one occasion he had reconstructed the image of the girl standing on the balcony, arrayed in her goddess gown of white silk, gold Baroque bracelets on her lean wrists. Now, examining her peasant's costume, he had to admit that it suited her just as well.

Brendan, being completely ignorant of his son's romantic past, or his present, for that matter, misinterpreted Hugh's nostalgic smile and elbowed him in the side.

"Just look at her! This surely is no Alison O'Mara. Wouldn't you like to trap such a bird in your net?"

"That particular bird is for contemplating only," Hugh replied with a sigh. "I pity the man who falls for her. But what is she doing here, in the Fenian camp?"

In reality, Hugh knew exactly what Isabel was doing there, but he was curious to hear his father's version of the story.

"Isabel is Aidan's daughter," Brendan declared slowly and solemnly, as if he were initiating his son into some exclusive mystery. "I bet she's lookin' for a husband among her father's lads. Look how she toys wi' them. Amusin' as hell! I've seen her in a saddle once, an intimidatin' sight for a man, dare I say. She can also down a glass of whiskey without takin' a breath. With all that, she's a perfect lady. Her father, Aidan McCormack, is nothin' to sneer at himself. I wouldn't mind becomin' kin with him. That would surely enrich our bloodline. Go, Hugh, talk to her."

Having spotted the three guests, the girl stopped laughing and removed the drunken young Fenian's hands from her waist.

"*Dia duit*," she greeted them with a slight bow and gestured for them to follow.

"*Dia's Muire duit*," Brendan replied under his breath, embarrassed by the rustiness of his Gaelic.

He could spend the eternity replaying her flawless greeting in his head.

Walking by her side, he could not help marveling at her gait, so firm and at the same time noiseless.

"How's your father, Isabel?" Brendan continued questioning her, seeking every excuse to maintain a dialogue with her.

"Full of hopes," she replied. "Thanks to my mother, we received more recruits this year than expected. She has a talent for directing young boys' hearts onto the right path. Another insurrection is not too far away, and we all await it anxiously, except for Count Markiewicz, of course. He threatens to fetch his son and return to his native Poland, never to see us again. Apparently, he wishes no part in this barbaric slaughter. That is how he refers to our endeavors. Can you conceive of it, Mr. Malone? And I had once thought the Count a wanton spirit! Never again shall I trust a continental artist. They make fickle allies. At any rate, I shall not beg the Count to stay. His loss! He shall miss a magnificent theatrical performance free of charge. What a shame! If only he would stay and take meticulous notes, perhaps he could bring revolution to Poland, too. It is about time our Polish brothers gnashed their teeth at their immediate neighbors. Imagine, a fine Catholic country trapped between Orthodox and Protestant savages. Don't you share my opinion on this matter, Mr. Malone?"

Brendan nodded fervently, even though he knew next to nothing about Poland and its neighbors. He would agree to anything that girl uttered, if only to keep hearing her indignant soprano.

"Well-said, Isabel! Whence you do derive such wisdom?"

"From you, of course! I'm blessed indeed. Some girls don't even have one father, while I have three. Aidan gave me life, the Count gave me wealth, and you, Mr. Malone, gave me wisdom. Fortified with such gifts, how can I lose?"

Unable to control a sudden onslaught of tenderness that was not entirely paternal in nature Brendan, squeezed Isabel's face with his callused hands and stamped her forehead with a kiss. The girl humored him, neither resisting nor returning the affection. She was accustomed to receiving spontaneous idolatrous kisses on various parts of her body.

"May God keep you," Brendan whispered, having pried his lips off her forehead. "I'll never forget your words to me. I could kiss you for eternity. But I fear it wouldn't please your Dadaí."

***

Truth be told, Aidan McCormack could not care less who kissed his daughter. He fully trusted Isabel to be the guardian of her own chastity, if chastity indeed was her endeavor. Having taught the girl how to dispose of persistent undesirable suitors, he considered his paternal role fulfilled. Simply put, he could not give Isabel what he did not possess, nor would he chastise himself for it. It sufficed that the girl had inherited his profile and his ability to put on lean muscle. The circumstances of her birth did not keep him awake at night. After all, it was not his fault that the woman, whose fancy he caught, turned out to be the daughter of Sir Henry Gore-Booth, an Arctic explorer and baronet. If the young heiress thought Aidan handsome enough to pose for a portrait, who was he to deny her that artistic whim? If she believed in free love, the sort that transcends the social hierarchy, who was he to dissuade her? The last thing that Aidan questioned was his worthiness of Constance.

His hostility towards the British was not by any means universal. He had not hated them always, nor had he hated them all. In fact, some of the most generous handouts he had received in life came from the alleged enemy's side.

As a boy of twelve, Aidan was offered a servant's position at the Kenwood estate on the banks of the river Camlin in Longford. The patriarch of the family picked Aidan out of his siblings as one would a puppy, not because the boy was the eldest or the strongest, but because he was the most English-looking. Without any hesitation, the landlord cupped Aidan's chin, turned his face upward and sideways, made him say a few phrases and declared that "his diction and pronunciation were not beyond repair." Thus, Aidan McCormack became the property of the Kenwood dynasty, a great insult for his dead father and a great relief for his surviving mother.

It was to his employer's family that he owed his education and his manners, which he eventually turned into potent weapons. An Anglo-Celtic shape-shifter, he was able to play up or down his Irish accent based on what the given circumstances demanded and navigated freely between the two worlds.

He wore his hair in the versatile fashion of the day. In the back it was cropped short to flaunt his long powerful neck. In the front he sported a luxurious forelock that could be pomaded and slicked back for more obliging occasions or ruffled and pulled forward when Aidan addressed his Republican brothers. That tuft of graying hair hanging over the forehead added drama to a rebel's image and was perfect for casting inflammatory glances into the audience. During Aidan's passionate tirades, the forelock would sway back and forth like a flag.

Being a centre of a Fenian circle did not hinder Aidan from joining the British Army and fighting in the Second Boer War in 1899 in Transvaal. The surest method to learn the enemy intimately was to spend some time fighting on the enemy's side. It also gave Aidan an opportunity to observe the resistance tactics of another nation colonized by the crown. It was in South Africa that he witnessed the phenomena known as "concentration camps" and "scorched earth". The knowledge he acquired over the course of that campaign was well worth the trip to the most remote tip of another continent, and the skull injury he sustained in one of the battle.

Now, age forty-five, he spent most of his time in his log cabin on the banks of the Shannon. The war injury had doomed him for a lifetime of chronic headaches and heightened sensitivity to light and sound. Aidan needed to be cautious about expending his strength. His mission was not to actively lead, but rather to inspire and instruct.

Several times a year he received visits from Constance, who remained his main liaison to Dublin and the affluent scholarly crust. She directed her most promising boys from *Na Fianna Eireann* to him. Aidan's camp in Carrick was the ultimate destination for those candidates that Constance hand-picked herself.

Thus, the former lovers worked towards the same goal; he, from his log cabin in the woods, and she, from in her mansion on Frankfurt Avenue. Their goal was to infiltrate and infect all circles of the Irish population, to shorten the gap between the working class and the intellectuals.

Lethargic, subtly nostalgic tenderness marked their reunions, finding outlet in the intertwining of fingers, smoothing of the hair and touching of the foreheads. There was only one bed in Aidan's cabin, so they would sleep on it, side by side, without undressing.

Sometimes Constance would bring medicine from the city to treat Aidan's headaches, but he would inevitably misplace it and later blame the head injury for his forgetfulness. Both would laugh.

Those caresses and gestures of concern posed no threat to Aidan's spiritual freedom or to Constance's marriage. The Count knew about her visits to Carrick and never expressed any objections. More than that, he looked forward to his wife's departures, as they provided him with a sorely needed break from the political meetings. The house on Frankfurt Avenue swarmed with poets and revolutionaries. The situation was growing more extreme with each passing year. After a while, this perpetual Celtic tempest would wear out even a romantic like Count Markiewicz. Since Constance had accepted his son Stanislas from the first marriage, the Count had no choice but to accept Isabel, who in the end, proved to be more of an amusement than a burden. The articulate dark-haired imp soon found a place in her stepfather's heart, and his will.

Then, somewhere in their incredible travels, the spouses produced another child together. The Count had a vague recollection of it being a daughter by the name Maeve, who in the end was conveniently dispatched to live with the Gore-Booth grandparents. In all fairness, the house of Frankfurt Avenue was not the most suitable place for an infant. This arrangement made absolutely no sense, and the Count did not even pretend that he understood it, but it seemed to satisfy everyone, at least the adults involved. Constance would be lying if she said that she longed for her youngest daughter. Maeve's birth had brought on a severe attack of postnatal melancholy that only intense political activism could cure.

Thus, little Maeve, conceived in the spousal bed, wound up being all but an orphan, while Isabel, a luscious fruit of illegitimacy, had pocketed two fathers; the Polish Count and the Irish rebel. Each doted on her in his own way, and neither one volunteered to assume the role of a disciplinarian. The girl grew up ignorant of patriarchal oppression. She viewed men purely as playmates and comrades-at-arms.The thought of being subordinate to one of them seemed inconceivable to her. If anyone hinted to Isabel about feminine duty and obedience, she would not even grow indignant. She would simply break into her melodic, bewitching laughter.

***

When Aidan saw his daughter escorting the three guests, he flung his arms open, as if endeavoring to fly.

"Brendan, I was just recalling you!" he exclaimed. "I thought, here's one man who'd leap with joy for us. Look at the lads we got this year, and most are under twenty! And those," he nodded at Dylan and Hugh, "are yours, I take it?"

"S'pposedly mine," Brendan replied, throwing a menacing glance at his youngest. "At least one of them. Not so sure about the other."

"Grand!" Aidan rubbed his hands together. "You couldn't have chosen a better time. Shall we commence?"

Aidan's last words made Hugh nervous.

"And what exactly are we going to commence?" he whispered to his brother. "I don't like the sound of it. What on earth is he talking about?"

"I don't know," Dylan muttered. "You better ask the chieftain."

But Aidan had already vanished, leaving only his daughter.

"Miss McCormack," Dylan began timidly, as he had not known her as intimately as his younger brother did.

"Please, call me Isabel," she requested. "We must do away with those courtly formalities, especially after your stellar performance under my balcony!"

Dylan blushed, recollecting that night in 1908 and his rendition of "God Save Ireland", which became a subject of many jokes among his classmates.

"You still remember, Miss McCormack?" Dylan slapped his forehead. "Forgive me, I meant to call you Isabel."

"How could I forget my Manchester Martyr?" She then turned to Hugh and graced him with her classical conspiratorial smile. "And you, Green Sleeves? I am tickled to see you here among us. I had a premonition that we would meet again in this life. I assume it means that you have experienced a change of heart?"

Hugh parted his lips, formulating an objection, but the girl did not give him a chance to speak up. Her muscled arms and her glossy black hair wrapped around his neck, choking him. Suddenly, Hugh came close to an unsettling epiphany. He began wondering if he had been deceived for the past two years. Perhaps, he was not Isabel's chosen, unconditionally beloved friend after all, but merely one of countless boys that she had enticed in this manner. All her alleged interest in his philosophy and her even supposed acceptance of his unionist inclinations, all that was pure pretense, a means of luring him to her side. This was where she ultimately wanted them, in her father's camp.

"Please, allow me to explain," he muttered, struggling to chase away that blasphemous suspicion, as his heart still wanted to believe in Isabel's sincerity. "I did not come here to—"

Again, she silenced him.

"How I prayed for this, my dear Hugh," she whispered, covering his mouth with her alabaster fingers. "The Brotherhood can't survive without a Latin scholar."

Still embracing Hugh, she glanced over her shoulder at Dylan, having remembered that he had an unanswered question.

"So, what were you going to ask, my lamb?"

"What exactly is your father preparin' for us?"

"Oh, just a modest ceremony," Isabel replied, toying with the loose ends of her braid. "All new members receive one after giving the Oath.

Hugh shuddered and drew back from Isabel, his suspicions having been justified.

"Dadaí told us nothing about it!" he exclaimed. "I was not prepared for any oaths. I thought we'd be meeting a few of his friends."

Isabel laughed, having interpreted his indignation as anticipatory anxiety.

"He must've wanted to surprise you."

"Well, he certainly succeeded! I do not like surprises of this sort."

At that moment Aidan returned, leading about fifteen more Fenians who immediately formed a semi-circle. After 1867 the initiations became more ceremonious, with more witnesses present.

Since the Fenians were not in the position to expend their energy on actual battles, they threw it wholly into their rituals.

"Mark my word, Mr. Malone, this is the biggest crowd we've had yet," said Basil Costello, one of the oldest members of the group. "When I was sworn in, there were ten of us. We took turns climbin' an empty barrel and then dispersed. How I envy your lads."

Aidan positioned Brendan's sons before the group and addressed everyone. "Dear comrades, we have extraordinary news. These two young fellows will join us today. They're already brothers in blood, and soon will be our brothers in spirit as well. Dylan, Hugh, I pray that you never doubt the righteousness of your choice. Our nation, that has been dormant for centuries, needs your courage and determination."

Hugh's face darkened, his eyebrows contracted, as he squeezed Dylan's hand, whispering, "What sort of circus is it? Dadaí dragged us here and didn't even ask our consent."

Dylan, who had been absorbing Aidan's words reverently, tried to free his hand.

"For God's sake, Hugh, not now," he hissed with annoyance. It means the world to Dadaí. Can't you do somethin' his way for once?"

"For once?" Hugh squeezed his brother's wrist even tighter. "My whole life has been one act of surrender after another, and I'm quite fed up with it."

"Oh, hush up! Couldn't you choose a better time to rebel against Dadaí?"

The subdued altercation between the brothers went unnoticed by the Fenians, as they all were staring at their charismatic chieftain. Aidan McCormack took out a scroll of parchment and handed it to Dylan who, as the eldest one, had the honor of pledging first. Throughout the history of the Republican Brotherhood there existed a few versions of the oath, both in Gaelic and English. Constantly amended and embellished, it became almost a folkloric piece. The one that ended up in Dylan's hands ran as follows:

In the presence of Almighty God, I do solemnly swear allegiance to the Irish Republic now virtually established; and that I will do my very utmost, at every risk while life lasts, to defend its independence and integrity and, finally, that I yield my implicit obedience in all things not contrary to the laws of God to the commands of my superior officers. So help me god. Amen.

It was one of those rare moments in Dylan's life when he thanked silently and sincerely his college professors who forced him to improve on his reading skills. Peering into the dark parchment, he uttered the words of the Oath almost without stammering.

Isabel reappeared, carrying a saber that she buckled to Dylan's belt, then placed her hands on his shoulders and kissed him on each cheek. *Failte...*

Dylan circled the applauding Fenians with his eyes, searching for his father's face. From the movement of Brendan' lips he understood, *Well-done, chieftain.*

"Well-done, indeed," Aidan McCormack confirmed aloud. "Now go on and pass the parchment to your brother."

When the scroll appeared before his eyes, Hugh drew back, hands locked behind his back, which instantly caused the applause and the howling to cease.

"What's the matter?" Aidan inquired, his face suddenly elongated. "Why won't you give the Oath?"

"Because I don't want to break it." Hugh spoke rapidly, with his face lowered, avoiding eye contact with his father. "And break it I shall—sooner rather than later. It is only a question of time."

Aidan managed to maintain his composure, even in the face of such an extraordinary confession. His posture and tone of voice communicated more curiosity than anger.

"My dear boy, where exactly are you heading with this?" he inquired, approaching Hugh. "You've traveled such a long way, and now you display such obstinacy. In God's name, explain yourself."

"I suppose, I have no choice," Hugh replied, exhaling, as the most difficult part of the confession was over; now he could glance up at his would-be comrades and even his father. "Please, know I am not motivated by contempt. I esteem your cause, even though I don't share your beliefs. I already gave my promise, to a woman, my wife. You would consider her your enemy, as she is English and a Protestant. Enough said? Perhaps, I haven't been an obedient son, but at least, I've been an honest one. Well, there's no more for me to say."

When Hugh departed, not a single head turned in his direction. No such thing had ever been recorded in the history of the Brotherhood. And least of all, one would have expected to hear such words from the son of Brendan Malone. Even Dylan, who harbored no illusions about his younger brother's patriotic sentiments, had not expected such a blunt rebellion. He blinked and pinched himself several times to make certain that he was not dreaming. Every time he opened his eyes, he was still standing on the same spot of the clearing, surrounded by the astounded Fenians. They were all staring at him, expecting an explanation, as he was the only Malone left in their sight. Brendan had also disappeared from the crowd.

Laden with all sorts of disagreeable premonitions, Dylan headed towards the stables and then, from the darkness of the chilly, moldy cabin, heard his father's voice.

"Well, son, better start prayin' now."

"Christ, have mercy!" Hugh exclaimed, in no way intending to pray. "Isn't Dylan enough for you? Look at what you've done to the poor devil. He doesn't hold a thought of his own. He doesn't fear dying, yet he's afraid of displeasing you. He'll never be a leader. That requires a brain and a free will, both of which you've snapped at the root."

Dylan struggled to absorb the meaning of those words. Though accustomed to the latent tension between his brother and his father, he could not recall them ever arguing in the open. More than that, Brendan had always been more reserved and formal with his youngest son than he had with anyone else.

Listening to the voices that seemingly belonged to people completely unfamiliar to him, Dylan remained on the same spot.

"You can't change anything," Hugh spoke. "Edith is my wife. It's a done deal. We're married."

"By whom, dare I ask?"

"A church."

"A Protestant church, I take it?"

"What's the difference?"

"Don't play an idiot with me. You *know* the difference damn well."

"All I know is what Father O'Malley has taught us, but I still don't see the difference. The majority of enlightened, civilized men don't see it."

"Father O'Malley has also taught that sins come in batches, and you're a livin' proof of that. Twice a traitor! First your race, and then your creed?"

"I have no creed!" Hugh shouted, elongating the vowels of the last word. "And neither have you, Dadaí! Yes, I've heard you blast and mock your holy Catholic Church a hundred times, while father O'Malley wasn't listening. You're only Catholic when it suits you, which is what most Catholics do at any rate. So, please, don't start arraying yourself in scarlet robes."

Brendan ignored Hugh's last comment. His arms crossed on his chest, he kept shaking his head.

"Congrats, my son! But tell me now, how did they lure you to their side? It can't all be over some perfumed slut who bewitched you. There must be more. I know how greedy for fame you are. So, what exactly did they promise you? A seat in the Parliament? Or will you settle for scraps from their plates?"

"They gave me everything that I've been lacking in my own home," Hugh replied, and his voice faltered. "You've been mainly preoccupied with your crops and taxes and your absurd charity cases. You think that by cajoling families into staying in Ireland, you are doing such a great service to them and the country? They would probably have a better chance somewhere else. Anywhere but here! Now you are toying with the Brotherhood, as a diversion from your provincial routine. Look at yourself, Dadaí! What a dull childhood you must have had. Have you not played your share of war games? Have your fancies changed since you were twelve? You want your sons for playmates. You dote over your tenants as if they were helpless infants, yet you would feed Dylan and me to the wolves only to prove to your friends what a patriot you are. Ever since we were born, you've been pushing us steadily towards the gallows. That is precisely where you want us, hanging in plain sight, your very own Manchester Martyrs. Oh, that would surely impress your Republican mates. Perhaps, they would compose a ballad in your honor; Brendan Malone, the selfless father who sacrificed his sons for the Cause! You have no use for me, Dadaí. I don't dance to your fiddle. I don't fit into your tapestry of Fenian grandeur. I wasn't a sturdy red bull like Dylan, so naturally I didn't count for much. I was ugly and feeble, an eyesore, a disgrace to your lineage. If not for my big brother, I would've been battered to pulp by the neighborhood goons. Thanks to that English family, that has since become my new family, I feel like a human being for once."

"My family…" Brendan mocked him, dragging out the letter "f". "They are laughin' their bloody heads off that you, such a vain idiot, hopped straight into their trap." Suddenly his voice became gentler. "Dear boy, for once in your life, listen to your father, who wishes no further harm to befall you. I know well what came over you, believe me. You went a little mad for an instant. Who wouldn't? A big city, false friends, false promises… It must've seemed so true to a poor village lad. I, too, made a mistake, a much graver one, by having sent you to Dublin, having tossed you into their midst. I should've known you'd break, untaught peasant boy that you are. I, too, had been a vain idiot. Admittin' to that, I'll be happy to forgive you this momentary cloudin' of the brain, if come with me right now and do what is expected of you. Your brothers are on that clearin', waitin' and prayin' for you. Does it mean nothin' at all? Sixteen years of your life passed among them. What you've left behind in the city, 'tis all but a lie. You've got time yet to denounce it. After all, 'twas only a Protestant church that wedded you. That marriage isn't worth much. Theirs is a fake religion created to justify adultery. Their rituals aren't recognized by Rome. Poor child, I've lived longer than you. They've proven to be our enemies, and there's no way 'round it."

Hugh did not respond immediately. For a second, Dylan thought he heard his brother laugh.

"I am beating my head against the wall," Hugh said at last. "What in the world made me think you'd understand? All that hatred you talk about was invented by stubborn sheep, Irish and English alike. They love to think they're fighting for some noble cause. Apart from it they don't feel worthy. Look carefully, Dadaí, if your eyes still can see, here's a land with no future. You live on it only because even our British neighbors don't want it, as it cannot sustain any crop other than potato. Spuds 'n whiskey, that's all the local men know. But behind those rotting fences there's a world I want to see."

"This rottin' fence is your motherland, and don't pretend 'tis not. You won't have another one."

"No, what I won't have is another life."

"That life isn't yours, not entirely. I gave it to you."

"So take it back! Go right ahead and shoot me, Dadaí, like you always say. That'll solve everything. All your troubles will end with one single shot. It will be just you, your Republican brethren, your voiceless wife and your brainless son."

Another pause followed. Dylan blinked and leaned his pounding head against the shutter.

"You know how cross I am when I speak in this voice," Brendan whispered. "I'm not sure how long I can hold up. Get the bloody hell away now."

Hugh left the stables silently, dragging his horse by the reigns. Dylan rushed to him, the whites of his eyes flashing frantically in the dark, and caught his brother by the sleeve.

"Wait now, Hugh! What's with you? Why did you say all that? Was the devil pullin' your tongue?"

Hugh continued dragging his horse, without even looking at his brother.

"Dadaí wanted to know the truth," he said in a flat, expressionless voice, "so I gave it to him, all of it. But I've shamed him enough for one night. Time has come for me to go."

Dylan suddenly removed his hand from his brother's shoulder.

"Spuds 'n whiskey, so that's what you think of us, baby brother? Answer me, is it true? God, here's one thin' I never thought I'd hear you say..."

Hugh found no words for reply, feeling a sudden sting of pity, if not of remorse. Poor Dylan! He did not always fully comprehend the course of events, but he never failed to suffer for others. And now he could not decide who was merited more compassion, Hugh or Dadaí.

"Look, Dylan, what happened here today has no bearing on our kinship. You're still my brother."

"Your brainless brother, the red bull! Remember?"

Hugh lingered next to him for a few seconds, then sighed and dove into the murky shrubbery.

Unable to raise his hands for a prayer, Dylan fell to his knees, his fists pushing into the dry pine needles. "God, mercy and save him!"

In 1910, summer apparently decided to bypass Northern Ireland altogether. The first weeks of June resembled those of March, only wetter and darker. Hail had pounded the soil to the core and turned the country roads between Belfast and Londonderry into orange swamp, making traveling impossible. For weeks, neither sun nor moon could be seen through the fog that engulfed the entire city including houses, carriages and horses. Even the most cheerful of hearts were driven into gloom.

"God must be awfully peeved," Edith Ashley sighed, turning her eyes to the window, and rested her sewing on her knees. "He's been shedding tears for the past two weeks."

"Nonsense, my dear," her father objected. "Never attribute human weaknesses to the Creator, and never resort to such embarrassing pseudo-poetic clichés. You have too much taste and too much common sense for that."

"I wasn't thinking of poetry, father."

"Still, the Almighty's tears are but a foolish superstition," the professor insisted.

"Oh, here comes the Almighty again!" John, Edith's younger brother chuckled from behind his Daily Gazette. "Or perhaps, it's another apocalyptic flood. Some of the most glorious events begin with a rain. One never knows. And don't you start fighting me, Edith. I'm an unredeemable heretic, which happens to be one of my most attractive traits. I've had plenty of theological debates with the Potato Prince, who now is our dear brother-in-law. And, since we mentioned the honorable Malone family, I hope Hugh won't ruin the picture that Papa had painted in his recommendation letter to Mr. Clayton. Let's hope Hugh wears a suit with all buttons in place and does not swallow the words' endings. I doubt that Mr. Clayton would appreciate the rich, flavorful Roscommon accent."

Awaiting no reply from his sister, John folded his newspaper and left the living room, smirking at his own wit. The professor suddenly remembered that he had a stack of student essays waiting for him in his study, so Edith was left alone.

The wretched weather had kept her inside all day. She could not even go to the house of Mr. Kent, the banker whose children she taught piano, yet idleness posed no threat to her, as there was no shortage of chores inside the house. Somebody needed to mend her younger sisters' dresses that were tossed in a motley pile on the table. Her fingers were already bleeding from constant stitching. The former star of the conservatory had to assume Cinderella's role.

One thing gave her a brief infusion of optimism each time she looked down on her hands — a thin belt of gold around her ring finger. It was presented to her by the man she called her husband, struggling to resurrect her features in her mind. Had it not been for the gold band, Edith could have sworn that everything that happened two months ago was but a blurry dream, and her husband was a ghost.

She had first seen Hugh during one of her customary visits to Dublin. Richard Ashley, although he called himself a Belfast resident, spent nine months of the year in Dublin, in a small flat near the University College where he taught philosophy. And Edith, who remained in Belfast with her younger sisters, was expected to visit him and make his widower's abode more habitable.

One evening, when they were strolling near the Stephen's Green, a student approached them and handed some manuscript to the professor. Edith eventually learned that the document was a dissertation on Rene Descartes, and the young man was the rising star of the philosophy department, Hugh Malone.

Their first encounter could hardly be described as romantic or even remotely intimate. The professor, prone to being easily distracted, began conversing with his student, having forgotten about his daughter's presence. No formal introductions were made that evening. Edith had remarked, however, even in the twilight, that the young man's expression was earnest and decisive, which contrasted the alarming fragility of his body.

She saw Hugh again a few days later at her father's flat where philosophy students gathered for tutoring and discussion twice a week. They all laughed at different political jokes and smoked different sorts of tobacco, but all shared the same reverence for their professor, who, in the very beginning had banned all concepts of age-based hierarchy from his house and insisted on being addressed by his given name.

"I may be thirty years older than you," the professor declared. "What is this period of time to the world's history? Petty fractions of a second, unworthy of a mention! I've seen twenty-year old sages and eighty-year old fools. So, let us not insult each other with silly titles."

Those who flocked to Richard Ashley belonged to the new crop of self-made intellectual capitalists. Having brushed aside their less than prominent pedigrees, the young scholars stuffed their bookshelves with Socrates and Nietzsche. They dove into debates, never losing a certain degree of civility, applauding to objections, aiming not to achieve any sort of agreement, but rather to take the controversy to the highest, until everyone was out of breath, if not ideas.

Edith served them "academia brew", a mixture of black tea and watered-down coffee, faithful to her usual silence and wondered whether to leave or to stay. The jovial democracy of those gatherings appealed to her, but she doubted that the rule of equality extended onto her as well.

One evening she received an impression that Hugh Malone wanted her to stay. First he nodded and vacated his chair, inviting her to join the company. Then he interrupted the conversation and directed everyone's attention to her.

"We've heard everyone's opinions except for yours, Miss Ashley. Which ideal appears to you more unreachable: the one of Sage as presented by Epictetus, or the one of supermen as presented by Nietzsche?"

It took nearly half a minute for Edith to utter a word, but then she declared on one breath, "The day when Nietzsche reconciles with Epictetus will be the day of mourning for the philosophy departments at all major universities. There will be nothing left to discuss, and the professors will need to take up other trades."

John Ashley twisted his mouth sardonically and clapped his hands a few times.

"Well said, dear sister! Gentlemen, you've heard the lady speak. Consider the case closed."

"Not just yet, dear brother," Edith parried. "This is just the beginning." Red patches appeared on her cheekbones, making them appear higher. Her gray eyes narrowed and darkened, burrowing Hugh a sort of curious gratitude. Who was that scrawny dark-haired boy, and what possessed him to lure her into the conversation?

Then one evening the two of them spent several hours together, after the noise and the tobacco smoke had subsided. Hugh had volunteered to stay behind and help blot the puddles of "academia brew" off the table. They talked until the oil in the lamp burnt out. Edith barely remembered how the conversation started, feeling particularly exhausted that evening. Without changing out of her work clothes, she sat down at the empty kitchen table, and Hugh quietly joined her.

"I don't mean to seem obtrusive," he started after a few minutes of silence, "but it troubles me to see you so forlorn. I surmise that you can smile, and that you desire to. So what is hindering you?"

Elbowing aside all notions of good manners, Edith answered Hugh's question, in more words than she intended to and without any expectation of sympathy.

"I had once studied to be a concert pianist in London. Three years ago my mother had taken ill and died within a month. Besides, the family house in Belfast needed a keeper, so I was forced to leave the conservatory and seek employment as a music teacher instead. Somebody had to look after my younger sisters while our Papa and John were in Dublin. You see, Papa did not wish to hire a governess and introduce a perfect stranger into the house, even though he had the means. He deemed his youngest daughters fragile. They were nine and seven at the time, and they had never been on their own or done anything for themselves, and I was already twenty-one. The men in my family presumed I was able and willing to shoulder the task of raising the girls. Of course, Papa found the arrangement perfectly convenient. God bless him! His progressive democratic ideals clearly did not apply to me. They did not prevent him from curtailing my performing career. He supports the ambitions of his students, but not those of his own daughter. I am yet to experience his generous side. Apparently, my dreams are a small price to pay for his domestic comfort. Dare I complain?"

"Do not complain," Hugh said, lowering his fist on the tabletop. "Protest!"

"Yes, I should have protested, three years ago. It's too late now. Nobody at the conservatory would know who I am anymore. But at some point, believe it or not, I was known as one of the most promising future performers. I have gotten a tantalizing taste of what could have transpired and what never shall. I admit I lack Christian humility. Crucify me for that! I find no comfort in sacrificing for the common good. Right now I am probably more useful than I ever was before, but that realization does not comfort me. It's far worse than one tragic event from which one inevitably recovers. It's the habit of denying yourself over and over again one thing that was the foundation of your pride. What am I worth in my own eyes now, with all my diligence wasted, my skill lost? My fingers don't move on the keys like they did before. Each year they grow a little stiffer, sloppier. The men in my family don't believe that I have sacrificed much. My frustration mystifies them. My father and John keep reminding me that I still have my piano students. One hell of a consolation prize! Pardon the profanity. Can I expect them to understand what it's like after having played Mozart and Bach, to be forced to teach those spoilt, untalented brats to carry a tune with one finger? Above all, their parents see no difference between a music teacher and a housekeeper. Both are hired help, both equally dispensable."

Edith traced the chipped edge of the empty cup with the tip of her finger.

"A dutiful woman ought to be in love with her shackles, or at least pretend to be," she continued. "That was how Mama had lived, martyring her talents and secretly hoping to see her eldest daughter fall into the same pit. On the surface, she encouraged me to pursue my musical passion, but in her heart she resented me. She always made sure that her heart attacks coincided with my performances. Then she died. Life continues, for everyone else, that is. My sisters keep on giggling, John keeps on reading his Daily Gazette, and Papa keeps running his little free-thinkers club. Tell me, what is there for me to anticipate in the next ten years? I'm the first one to awaken in the morning, and I don't even care if the sun shines or not. I know for sure that it doesn't shine for me. I catch myself thinking that nothing is for me any longer, and that's frightening."

Edith suddenly paused and shook her head, wrapping her fingers tighter around the cracked cup. "I am well aware that my behavior is abominable, Mr. Malone. I should not be telling you any of this."

"And why on earth shouldn't you, Miss Ashley?" Hugh asked. "Remember, I was the one who coerced you into this confession."

"But I should not have given into the temptation," Edith insisted sternly. "I have always been taught that it distasteful to pour one's soul before strangers. There are girls who are always cheerful. Take the Kent sisters, for instance. Each time I go to their house to give their little brother a piano lesson, I always run into them. Not only do they dress in the latest fashion, they know just the proper things to say. I've never seen either one sulk. Everyone admires them."

"Yes, I have met specimens of the breed to which you refer," Hugh affirmed, with a fatigued, all-knowing nod. "But why must you compare yourself to them? Who knows what they would do in your place! It's easy to chirp and say the proper things when one's family rolls in money."

"Even so… When Mama was still alive, she said that a lady must never burden others with complaints. Perhaps, I'm immune to good manners. The more I keep silence, the more I yearn to scream. I try to be composed and polite, but some tiny demons tickle my throat from the inside, forcing out profanities. Sometimes I want to set the whole world on fire. See, I go at it again! If I went to church, I could bother a minister, but I haven't been religiously disposed in the past two years. Thus, I'm bothering you instead."

Hugh took the chipped cup from her hands for fear that Edith would inadvertently cut herself. An injury of this sort would make it difficult for her to play piano. She shuddered from this unexpected brushing of fingers, but did not take her hand away. Her eyelids suddenly felt heavy from the too long-restrained tears, and keeping the eyes open became nearly impossible. She bowed her head and sat silent for some time.

"Don't apologize," Hugh said finally, "at least, not to me. I have also been taught a great many things. I am still struggling to toss them out of my head. How do you dispose of all the useless, cumbersome gifts you have received over the years?"

Edith lifted her head and straightened out.

"Well, you've listened to me enough. Now I'd like to hear your story, as much as you're willing to share."

"I have no secrets, and my story is hardly the stuff of which legends are made. As you must already know, I'm a son of a petty landowner. At seventeen I came in the Dublin with my older brother. We were both born in 1888 – he in January, and I in December. God bless our poor mother! Sometimes I joke that we were born in the same year, but not in the same family. At any rate, we, natives of Roscommon and practically peasants, found ourselves among boys with golden pocket watches. As you can imagine, those boys did not hurry to welcome us. It was a shock for poor Dylan. What, someone did not rush to kick football with him? Unaccustomed to this sort of rejection, he started a few fist fights and, consequently, was branded a savage."

Edith watched the reemerging memories sharpen Hugh's features. In the beginning of their acquaintance this opinionated, seemingly invulnerable young erudite struck her as someone incapable of holding a grudge against life.

"Miss Ashley," he continued, "you have mentioned the girls who frequent reception halls and receive praise regardless of what they say or do. You should've seen some of my classmates! During lectures, they applied every effort to demonstrate their boredom, yet they still received unconditional praise from their teachers, mostly for bearing their father's surnames. The dullest and the laziest were patted on the head for each half-coherent word, and I had to exert myself ten times harder to be taken seriously. Your father was the only professor who considered me worth his time. The rest couldn't care less, since my father held no tangible authority. All he could give them was a sack of half-rotten potatoes and a few sturdy workhorses.

"For the first two years my brother and I were equally miserable. Then our uphill paths began to split. Dylan discovered comfort in pubs, and I turned to books. I read anything that I came across in the philosophy section of college library: Plato, Descartes, Humes. Yes, I still had my books."

"And I had music!" Edith exclaimed, even though it was not her intention to reroute the course of the conversation back to herself. "Those men who've been dead for centuries were dearer to me than those around me. I spent three perfectly blissful years in the conservatory. Solitude and a good piano—I needed nothing else. I lost it all as soon upon my return to Belfast. That two-storey plaster box where we lived never was much of a home to me, and my father... Well, let's just say he was a father to his younger children, not me."

"Miss Ashley, you haven't met *my* father," Hugh said, shaking his head. "It kills me to see what he's done to himself. By nature he is loyal, honest, generous, and not entirely deprived of intelligence, but he had invested his all of his strength into a dead-end cause. He's been an IRB member for almost quarter of a century, and he hopes that my brother and I will join him."

"What is your prediction?" Edith asked. "Will your father's dream come true?"

"With Dylan it might. But I've always known that sooner or later I would have to disappoint Dadaí. A day will come when he will declare me a traitor. That title is given out quite liberally in our circle. I've had my entire life to prepare myself for that day. Dadaí holds his own view of fatherhood: *I gave you life, and therefore I can dispose of it the way I see fit.* He shall never understand that it's not my land that I denounce, but the madness that rules it. All the boys in Roscommon have been marked with the same brand. To them and Dadaí I was a creature fallen from the moon. The wisdom I found in my books holds no value in that circle. You will certainly appreciate the irony of my position, Miss Ashley. In college I was considered a provincial simpleton, and at home in Roscommon, a city snob. There has been no chance of me winning. I have been rejected by both camps."

"I have comforting news for you, Mr. Malone," Edith said. "Men who subscribe to the philosophy of the Enlightenment era do not need to belong to a camp. Noble, highly evolved beasts do not run in herds, but stand on craggy heights to watch the plains below."

"I was not lamenting my social station," Hugh corrected her delicately. "I was merely commenting on it. Still, the most disheartening spectacle was that of the girls in the Tulsk, pretty girls, all fated for the same future. At night they dreamed of lollipops, ribbons and ear-rings they would buy at the next town fair. Ah, the pinnacle of feminine ambition! All their imagination had been smothered over the course of their childhood. To think has become unnecessary, and to desire has become sinful. By the age of sixteen, most of those girls have turned into marriageable wooden dolls. Yet they giggle on!"

"And the thought of saving one has never occurred to you?" Edith asked. "Surely, a man like you would have his quixotic inclinations."

"God knows, I have tried, but every time I arrived too late. Too much damage had already been done. I courted them my own way, and they thought me a madman. You see, I did not buy them cheap earrings, nor I did not try to drag them into the hay barn like Dylan would. Ah, what's the use now? I don't intend on returning home or choosing my future wife from the women there, that's for certain. Call me foolishly optimistic, but I have not given up hope of finding a scholarly-minded young lady with an impressive collection of rare books for a dowry."

On that note they parted for the night. Edith, despite the unfamiliar feeling of relief, would not dare to assign any great significance to the conversation. At last, someone allowed her to speak without interruption, which by itself was more than she had grown to expect from other me in her life.

NINE: All The Blessings
In The World

Upon her return to Belfast, Edith discovered a letter waiting for her. The damaged seal indicated that her younger sisters had already made themselves familiar with the content of the envelope.

Dear Miss Ashley,
I hope you do not mind me writing to you. Your father was kind enough to give me your address in Belfast. I would like very much to continue our dialogue. Please, let me know when you will be in Dublin next. Perhaps, we could go to the theatre and watch the Countess Cathleen sell her soul to the devil.
Your friend, Hugh Malone

In this world there are things far more original than a few formal lines written in purple ink on a yellow sheet of paper. More than once Hugh had watched his college comrades improvise notes to their lady-friends inviting them to the theater or to a dance. He could not help scoffing at the anxiety invested into this seemingly mundane ritual that should not take more than a few minutes. And now the brilliant young scholar, who in the matter of six weeks had written a fifty-page dissertation on Descartes to be presented for adjudication before twelve philosophy professors, spent three days drafting and scrapping those four-and-a-half lines.

As for Edith, the transformation she had undergone after her last trip to Dublin left everyone around her perplexed. The pallid, perpetually tense girl, who spoke lowly through her teeth, suddenly discovered her ability to laugh. The corners of her mouth relaxed, and the premature crease between her flaxen eyebrows started to disappear.

Contrary to her sisters' conviction, Edith was not born to be homely. She simply did not believe in bright colors, jewelry, and all those feminine tricks upon which the other girls relied so heavily. At the age of twenty-four, she could easily pass for a thirty-year old in her straight plain frocks that only varied in the shades of gray. The only adornment she ever wore was a silver cross on a thin chain, but even that she hid under her clothes. The deceased Mrs. Ashley, preoccupied with her daughter's artistic and intellectual evolution, somehow overlooked such issues as fashion and rapport with young men. Edith had exactly five weeks to reverse her image.

When, at their next meeting, Hugh saw Edith in a gown of burgundy satin, with a garnet necklace around her neck, his eyes had to reacquaint with her before he greeted her properly. Edith smiled, savoring his confusion, and stretched her hand to him with the boldness she could barely fathom only two months ago.

They did go to see W.B. Yeats' acclaimed masterpiece. According to the rumor, the playwright himself attended each performance just to watch his beloved Maud Gonne on stage. The Abbey Theatre was an excellent place for unexpected encounters with some of the capitol's most distinguished Gaelic revivalists, including Lady Gregory and Sean O'Casey. The playwrights were honoring the memory of their colleague, John Mullington Synge, the author of the scandalous creation *The Playboy of the Western World*, who had died a year earlier of cancer.

***

Bulmer Hobson arrived in the company of the actress Molony, his first romantic interest worth mentioning. The fervent Fenian activist, who belonged to at least a dozen nationalistic and cultural organizations, half of which he had founded himself, had enjoyed mixed fortunes in his intimate life that had started surprisingly late. Hobson could recite most electrifying speeches before a crowd of four-thousand New Yorkers at the Grand Central Palace, yet his eloquence would abandon him, and his tongue would become paralyzed in the presence of a woman. Almost twenty-seven, Hobson was as clumsy and bashful with the opposite sex as Molony was bold and frivolous. For reasons that only made sense to him, Hobson thought of himself as unhandsome. In reality, he looked like a younger version of W.B. Yeats, with the same straight, slightly elongated nose and a generous, well-defined mouth.

Before embracing Irish nationalism, Hobson needed to disengage himself, however inconspicuously, from Quaker pacifism into which he was born. The perpetual conflict between his upbringing and his persuasion was creating premature creases on his high forehead. So far, the Irish nationalist in him appeared to be winning. Hobson was quickly gaining fortunes in the IRB, attracting new members with his boundless passion. If there were no new clubs for him to join, he would create one himself. Naturally, all those fascinating activities made it difficult for him to hold a paying day job. Prolonged unemployment spells that constantly sent him running to his parents in Belfast did not exactly contribute to his confidence as a suitor. "I am homely and impoverished," he would lament under his breath. "Whenever a beautiful woman rejects me, I start a new club or a newspaper to ease the pain." He must have experienced quite a few rejections, real or perceived, because the number of clubs and publications kept multiplying. The Ulster Debating Club, the Protestant National Society, the Hurling League, the Dungannon Clubs, the Ulster Literary Theater, Na Fianna Eireann, Freedom Clubs, *The Republic* newspaper — all those were the fruits of his romantic travesties. Whenever some new enterprise appeared up on the cultural map of Dublin or Belfast, it was safe to assume that another girl had failed to respond to Bulmer Hobson's smile.

It took a decisive, uninhibited female like Molony to break someone like Hobson out of his armor of self-loathing. In the foyer, before dozens of onlookers, she tousled his long forelock and tickled his chin, laughing gregariously, aiming to attract attention to their affair that was being rekindled after several months of separation. Helena's auburn locks were glittered and coiled up in a most decadent fashion, giving her a resemblance with a Roman senator's wife. The peacock feathers on her head wavered. Hobson blushed and shivered as someone half his age would. Suddenly, the actress rose on her tiptoes, squeezed her suitor's generously pomaded head and bit into his lips. It was not a mere kiss but some sort of a metaphysical ritual, a mystical, transformative manipulation. When Hobson finally separated his face from Helena's, he was a transformed man. From that evening on the foyer of the Abbey Theater was known as a place where frogs turned to princes.

Having witnessed the scene between the compulsive club-starter and his Bohemian muse, Hugh took Edith by the arm and leaned his head closer to hers. For once, the sight of another man's happiness did not trigger pangs of envy or resentment in him.

Hugh held a personal grudge against Hobson, whose behavior he apparently was expected to imitate. "Now why can't you be more like Bulmer?" Brendan would ask him. "It isn't Bulmer's fault that his parents are rich Protestants. If anythin', it makes his devotion to our cause all the more admirable. Such a staunch, self-assured, vocal young Fenian he is, a Northern gem! He plays Gaelic football and writes Gaelic poetry. He's the sort of son I'd be proud to have and show off to my mates. When will you write a book or start a newspaper? It can't be that difficult. I'm not payin' for your bloody education in vain. You better make friends with Bulmer, join every club of his and learn to be like him in every way."

No, Hobson definitely was not Hugh's favorite person in Dublin. Even if there had been a slight chance of the two becoming friends, Brendan had killed it at the root. Still, on that night at the Abbey Theater, Hugh was ready to embrace his unofficial rival and wish him all the luck in love and war.

While ascending the stairs onto the second level, Hugh spotted Isabel McCormack in the company of the two Pearse brothers. The eldest one, Patrick, still numb from the tragic death of his friend and alleged love interest Eveleen Nicholls, appeared oblivious to his surroundings. Theater-going was no longer his entertainment or even his solace, but rather a mere reflex, a habit he did not have the motivation to break. He dragged his feet wherever Miss McCormack led him. If she were to tell him to leap off the balcony, he would have complied without any questions. Patrick's spiritual condition was most fragile. He spent most of his days at St. Enda's, the bilingual school he had founded, raising the new crop of Irish-speaking boys, pondering out loud the romantic notion of dying for the Cause, reciting Gaelic poems in his ethereal, droning voice that had the power to enchant his students. Patrick's siblings and friends would take turns accompanying him to concerts and performances in the city. Everyone agreed that it would be dangerous to leave him alone for too long. For all they knew, he could start an uprising and persuade his pupils to die by his side. Heroic death akin to that endured by his mythical idol Cúchulainn, became his mistress. Patrick mumbled about it with the same fervor a normal man would mumble about a voluptuous woman who visited him in his dreams. Breathing ancient Celtic myths, he rebelled against modernity, realism, logic. The vulgar pedestrian diction in Synge's *Playboy* threatened Ireland's heroic past. It was disgusting how everyone at the theater worshipped that playwright just because he was dead. Oh yes, that instantly turned his mediocre skits into masterpieces. Well, Patrick Pearse would not bow to Synge! He was determined to boycott everything modern and secular. Even in daily conversations he favored archaic, bombastic expressions. Naturally, England was to blame for this poisonous influence.

"I would rather see Dublin in ruins than that we should go on as we are living at present," Patrick kept saying.

No wonder his well-wishers hesitated to leave him alone with his fantasies of a mass suicide. He seemed much too eager to realize them.

Willie Pearse, who barely remembered Hugh, simply passed by without a greeting, but Isabel, having seen her most successful pupil with a new lady on his arm, congratulated him with that smile reserved exclusively for her favorites who had seen the miniature art gallery inside her house on Frankfurt Avenue.

Hugh nodded gratefully and shifted his attention back to the one whose fingers entwined around his elbow like a carved ivory ring. He could hardly keep notice of what was happening on the stage, even though he was the one who had suggested seeing *Countess Cathleen*. Hugh was ashamed to admit that he used the invitation as a respectable excuse for a rendezvous. He had already seen *Countess Cathleen* at least three times. At that point, her fate no longer interested him. Everyone knew how the play concluded. Now Hugh could not wait for what seemed to be an agonizingly tedious performance to end, so he could finally be left alone with Edith. This wildly talented, articulate and willful girl was acquainted with the same anguishes as he.

Hugh's wandering thoughts kept returning to the kiss he witnessed in the foyer, the brazen, intoxicating lip-lock between the Gaelic activist and the frivolous young actress. That scene left a brighter impression on him than what was happening on the stage. Hugh imagined Edith and himself in the place of Molony and Hobson. At once, his lips began to tingle, and his jaw began to ache. Hugh had to cover the lower part of his face with his hand to settle the throbbing. He had not been kissed in two years, and now his body was punishing him for having neglected its needs. A boy does not thrive on academic research alone. Hugh's instincts seized him by the collar and gave him a good-natured shaking.

***

When the young couple walked out of the theatre, it was snowing for the first time that year. Large shapeless flakes collided in the lukewarm air and melted before even reaching the pavement. Instantly, Edith's velvet jacket became darker from the moisture, and her ash hair curled.

They left the noisy, lantern-lit streets behind and stepped into an alley. The snow clustering on their eyelashes blurred their vision. Hardly thinking of where they were going and with what purpose, they resembled a pair from the Hugh Goldwyn Rivere's painting "The Garden of Eden". Involuntarily, Hugh recalled his unforgettable stroll with Isabel McCormack down Frankfurt Avenue in 1908. Now, two years later, he was reliving the moment. The same city, a different street, a different woman…

There are moments in the early stages of budding love when the universe appears considerably more pleasant, because it does not transcend certain boundaries set by two souls that had recently discovered the pleasure of each other's company, bathing in the short-lived illusion of omnipotence.

***

Over the following two months Hugh and Edith did not have too many opportunities to be alone. Yet both noticed that with every meeting they talked less and less, not for the lack of things to say to each other, but because the necessity for words was decreasing. Even eye contact was no longer required. Neither one remembered when exactly they started addressing each other by their first names or how they kissed for the first time. They marked no memorable occasions, or rather, did not discriminate special from casual. Both were, to a certain degree, romantics, but not in the least sentimental.

For Richard Ashley, initiating heart-to-heart discussions with female family members did not come quite as naturally as delivering lectures. Nevertheless, one evening during his daughter's visit to Dublin, he summoned her into his study and made an honest attempt to have a long-overdue candid conversation.

"I did not know the extent of your unhappiness," he confessed, commanding himself to look Edith in the eye. "It simply eluded me. I admit that recalling you from London was an act of thoughtless cruelty. I should have allowed you to finish your studies. Your mother's death may have made me somewhat inattentive. For a time I found myself at a loss, disoriented. Believe me, it never was my intention to bury you. I know it is too late to remedy the situation. You have already lost three years."

"Please, do not force yourself to apologize, Papa," Edith replied. A spasm seized her temples, as she fought to drive the tears back inside. "Then I shall have to force myself to forgive you, and I am not certain I am quite ready for that yet," she continued lowly through her teeth, feeling her throat contract. "I know you need to unburden your conscience, but please, not now. Can't you see how hard I am trying to harness my anger? Yes, it's still quite raw. No more words, Papa! Spare me your apologies and disheartening reminders. Just revert to being your usual inattentive self and allow me to dwell on the single benefit that came out of my recall. Had you not forced me to leave the conservatory, had I not traveled to see you in Dublin, I never would have met Hugh."

"All right," Richard Ashley agreed faintly. "I shall pretend that this conversation had never taken place, if that would make your burden easier to bear."

"We'll simply have to live with our respective burdens, Papa. I shall live with my anger, and you with your remorse. Now, I believe your bookshelves need dusting."

Richard lifted his pale hand and made a dismissive, sweeping gesture.

"Those shelves are dusty indeed. And afterwards, why don't you make us some of your famous academia brew? I am expecting company tonight."

To the professor's credit, watching his star pupil court his eldest daughter, he remained a marvel of tact, wisdom and practicality. The rashness of the events did not seem to intimidate him. Of course, he could have dragged Edith through the conventional torments of receptions, courtship and three-year long engagements, for the sake of satisfying the sensibilities of his extended family. Fortunately, nature blessed him with a phenomenal amount of common sense. Looking at his prickly, withdrawn, defiantly unfashionable Edith who dreaded and despised events of this nature, the Professor carefully weighed her chances and decided that Hugh Malone was God's gift to her.

An Irishman, so what? The concept of nationality did not exist to those who aspired to enlightenment. A provincial, who cared? Hugh's rough edges were no more obvious than in any of the city boys. More than that, he did not have that intolerable air of giddiness so typical of the young bourgeois. To the hell with the meaningless pedigrees and the wealth earned by others!

Contrary to the custom that dictated that the suitor should first seek the permission to propose from the father of his prospective bride, Hugh and Edith informed the professor of their decision to marry. It was not Hugh's conscious intention to defy the custom; he simply was ignorant of it. Fortunately, Professor Ashley's knowledge of matrimonial etiquette was just as sketchy. It is not uncommon for an academician to be unaware of all social nuances. Hugh's faux pas came unnoticed and therefore unpunished. If anything, the professor would have found this act of audacity endearing.

In Hugh's defense, he never imagined that he would be proposing at the age of twenty-one, especially to a middle-class Englishwoman. It had not occurred to his parents to prepare him for such an occasion, as they seemed fairly convinced that marriage was not in the cards for him. Discussing such delicate matters with their poor weakling would be outward cruelty. It was always understood that Dylan would have a family. It was only a question of which girl he would deign to make the lucky bearer of his offspring. With Hugh, parents were less optimistic.

"Who would love him save for his mother?" Máirín would lament, not caring if the object of her maternal distress could hear her.

A few weeks before the wedding, while trying on his suit, Hugh examined his reflection in the mirror without reluctance, shame or disgust. Contrary to the remarks he had heard growing up, his back was not hunched over, and his legs were not crooked. In fact, his bones were rather well-formed. Granted, there was not much meat on them, but this minor flaw could be downplayed with a properly tailored suit.

His face was not homely either. Brushing a curling lock away from his eyes, Hugh took the unthinkable liberty of comparing his forehead to that of W. B. Yeats. A woman desired him! Not just any woman, a scholar's daughter, a pianist. His nosebleeds and wheezing spells did not repulse her. Those vexatious peculiarities of his body were not, as it turned out, some horrendous offenses that would doom him for a life of involuntary celibacy. He, Hugh Malone, was going to have an honest-to-God wedding night after all. Those who ridiculed and belittled him could burn in hell. This time he would surpass his own brother. There were countless secrets of the flesh that Dylan would never uncover with his peasant bride. Inexperienced as he was himself, Hugh still surmised that greater pleasures could be found in an English bedroom than in an Irish barn house. Between kisses that were growing longer and more elaborate, Edith planted certain images in Hugh's head, images that made the blood in his temples pound. So much for the notion of Englishwomen being stiff and prudish!

Three days before the wedding, they secluded themselves in a barren guest bedroom, with the dusty curtains drawn. They lay on an uncovered mattress, with pillows, knitted woolen throws and old books scattered on the floor. Little by little, the fantasies that had been brewing in Hugh's lively mind began materializing, with fervent encouragement from Edith. Hugh was certain that neither Donnie's Maggie nor Dylan's Caitlin even suspected of such tricks. They only knew how to give birth every eighteen months.

Feeling his ribcage expand with swirling hot fluid, Hugh plunged into self-indulgence, in defiance of his creed, of his origin. Two decades of relentless inferiority and self-loathing gave way to a carnal celebration. Edith, with her hair loosened and a giant encyclopedia placed under her lower back, did not resist the sudden assault. Their caresses went a bit farther than she had anticipated, and there would be not much left for the actual wedding night, but that seemed to be the pattern of their courtship. Everything else had been happening at an accelerated pace. She suspected that Hugh's passion contained an element of revenge, but she did not know how prevalent that element was.

Edith had her own scores to settle, namely with the married women her age who had begun sneering, referring to her as an old maid. Not that she had ever planned on remaining an old maid. She had entertained quite earnestly the idea of taking a lover, perhaps even more than one, should the institution known as traditional family shut her own. Perpetual celibacy was not a fate Edith was willing to accept. The mere thought of dying a virgin made her fingertips tingle. During her conservatory years, Edith befriended a number of free-spirited young gentlemen who had no intentions of having families and would not mind satisfying their appetites with a beautiful female colleague. For the past three years Edith had kept this possibility on the back of her mind. It kept her from throwing herself off the balcony. One day, when her little sisters would finally let go of her skirt, she could rejoin the cheerful circle of musicians back in London, a tiny Bohemian paradise which she had been forced to leave behind. One day she would rejoin her element and never make another sacrifice for the rest of her life. Yes, she would become that unashamed, promiscuous middle-aged woman with a harem of young boys from the conservatory and army of mangy cats. She already knew what colors those cats would be and how she would name them. She would wear a wide-brimmed hat with a veil and fox stole in the middle of June, and small children would recoil from her in fear, thinking her a witch. Yes, she would commit all those atrocities as a means of revenge for her stifled youth.

Relief had come to her sooner than she had anticipated. She would not need to resort to her alternative plan after all. The mangy cats and starving musicians could wait. She was lolling in the arms of a fervent Irishman three years her junior and as shameless as he was inexperienced. Having always taken pride in her flat stomach and white skin, Edith was grateful to have found a man who appreciated those traits.

After the breathtaking game in the shaded guestroom, it was a chore for them to straighten their wrinkled clothes, blot the sweat from their foreheads, smooth their hair and go downstairs, pretending that all that time they had been just looking at some old books. Luckily, John was out of the house that evening. Otherwise, he would have jumped at the opportunity to taunt them to death. As for the professor, he did not even raise his head when he heard the door upstairs slam. When he was in the middle of reading student dissertations, nothing short of a fire could get his attention.

There was one thing that seemed to be troubling Edith.

"What about your father?" she asked Hugh the next day. "How will he take the news? I have several good reasons to suspect that I am not exactly the daughter-in-law he dreamed about."

"He'll settle eventually," Hugh responded with a fatigued, dismissive shrug. "What choice does he have? I can't continue fashioning my life to his satisfaction."

Their wedding could hardly be called a ceremony, for it had passed so inconspicuously. The golden bands appeared a little too thin, but Hugh insisted on buying them with his own money, without any help from Professor Ashley. Such gesture of independence only elevated him in the eyes of his father-in-law and even of John who had the habit of taunting everyone and was impossible to impress.

"By the next Christmas we shall have a house," Hugh declared, "not an extravagant one, but our own. And the first thing brought inside that house will be a new grand-piano. Yes, you will perform again. I will see that your musical career is resurrected, even if I must halt mine."

A few days after the wedding, Edith returned to Belfast where her young husband was supposed to join her after graduating college and paying a visit to his parents in Roscommon. He had warned Edith not to wait for any letters from him, as the trip to his former home would be an unpleasant necessity.

***

Hugh arrived in the middle of June, somewhat earlier than expected. He greeted everyone jovially and did not release Edith from his arms, but his face appeared a little leaner than usual, and the gaze of his eyes framed by dark-olive circles seemed dissipated. When everyone sat down at the dinner table and John asked him how things were going in Roscommon, the fork in Hugh's hand shuddered.

"Very well, thank you. My parents send you their greetings."

The tremor in his hand was so slight, that nobody even noticed.

"And Dylan, does he grudge me still?" John would not stop interrogating his brother-in-law. "Come, tell me the truth, does he still curse me out?"

"Of course, he still curses you out. You've left quite an impression," Hugh replied, anxiously switching the topic and the tone of his voice. "I can't wait to meet Gerry Clayton and start working. I brought a fantastic Latin textbook with me."

Soon enough, Hugh assumed his duties. Gerry Clayton was the son of a Professor Ashley's university friend. Chronic illness of the lungs kept the boy from attending school, leaving his father no choice but to find a home tutor, and Hugh appeared to fit the position ideally. Mr. Clayton thought it was far better to deal with a young college graduate than with a professor who demands a raise after each new article he publishes. And Hugh, even if he lacked experience, could be reproached for lack of diligence. Seeing in the boy a reflection of his former self, Hugh quickly befriended his pupil and often stayed to talk with him after the lesson was over. Like the majority of weak, sickly children, Gerry exceeded his peers intellectually and grasped at ideas with no less vigor than other boys would grasp at a rugby ball. No small inspiration for any teacher.

Mr. Clayton, more than content with his choice, never hesitated to express his appreciation. He began introducing Hugh to his acquaintances in the Queen's College of Belfast, inviting him to seminars and banquets. Hugh lost the count of the hands he had shaken. Once during a reception, Mr. Warwick, the current centerpiece of the Belfast's intelligence, an author of countless philosophical pamphlets, approached Hugh to speak to him in person.

"I took my time to read your work on Descartes, and, I confess, it made quite an impression on me, even before your age was brought to my knowledge! Was there any particular reason, may I ask, why you chose Descartes?"

"He has been undeservedly neglected for the past few decades. Only because I sincerely believe that his philosophy can save the world. We don't have so many senses to merely accept what others tell us. It is not faith, but rather doubt that will bring us closer to God. Should the guardians of the Christian tradition set on a crusade against me, I shall accept the challenge most eagerly."

Standing in the corner of the reception room, a slender glass of wine in his hand, Hugh realized how irrevocably he had fallen in love with his new life. To mingle with people like Mr. Warwick, to discuss Descartes without receiving bewildered stares, to speak proper English without being thought a snob. Could there be a greater bliss? *Guardians of Christian tradition...* How naturally and smoothly those graceful little phrases rolled off his lips! How witty, sophisticated and relaxed he came across!

Having shared the phrase with Edith, Hugh caught himself dizzy with superstitious terror. He had gone a bit too far. It was raw arrogance screaming now, threatening to break his chest. Then he reminded himself that this arrogance was justly earned, that there was no harm in a little egotistic retribution. After all, did he not spend the last three years immersed in grueling studies? Did he not lay aside his heritage to be accepted by those brilliant men? Did he not quarrel with his father and miss his only brother's wedding? Now it was not only his right, but his duty to enjoy his new life.

"As I told you," Professor Ashley addressed him after the reception, "once you ascend to a certain level, the air seems cleaner. Beware, this world is a battlefield of its own, and the wars are fierce. Once your image of a debutant wears off, your colleagues will stop clapping you on the shoulder and start sinking their claws into you until you bleed. Prepare yourself for a merciless attack."

"Oh, I do not expect an easy life. Constant victories become inevitably boring. And there is no shame in being defeated by men like Mr. Warwick."

Just when Hugh thought that his satisfaction had crested, he received a letter from Isabel McCormack. He honestly did not expect such encouragement from her after his overt rebellion in her father's Fenian camp. To his pleasant astonishment, Isabel had actually taken the time to find his address in Belfast and personally congratulate him on his rapid rise to the academic Olympus.

I see my predictions came true, which does not happen too often. You revive my hope for humanity, dear Hugh. Our country has a greater need for sober minds than for flaming hearts. How glad I am now that I persuaded you to embrace Descartes. When you started a riot against your own father, I wanted to smother you with kisses, fond as I am of Mr. Malone. It is a pity that you left so hastily. As I said, it matters nothing to me whose side you are on as long as you have a good reason to be there. Keep allegiance to yourself, and you'll keep my friendship forever. Next time you are in Dublin, stop by my house. I'm positively dying to meet your wife.

The letter lifted Hugh's spirits, even though it contained a significant factual error: Isabel was the one who introduced him to Descartes. He was already well underway in his studies of the 17th and 18th century philosophers when they met. Still, if she wished to take credit for his brush with Enlightenment, Hugh would be willing to indulge her. He found it flattering, amusing and endearing that a woman of her caliber would want to feel like she had contributed to his success.

Urgent matters regarding his estate kept Brendan in Dublin for over a week in August. Who would have fathomed that such a small plot of infertile soil would require signing so many documents? Had it not been for the need to meet with his attorney, Brendan never would have gone to the city. The urban hassle, and particularly the multitude of the British on the streets, had been maddening him since the moment he stepped off the train. Dublin kept on changing for the worst year after year, gradually transforming into something insane, roaring and groaning.

As soon as the last office door had shut behind Brendan, he jumped on the train back home. But, even when the scenery behind the window became more familiar and appealing to eyes, when the slums and the factories changed into potato fields, his heart did not regain much of its former ease.

During his stay in Dublin, Brendan happened to pass by the University College that his sons had once attended. He had to squeeze his temples to force the reminder out of his head. He had not seen Hugh since June.

Over the past four years, Brendan had grown accustomed to lengthy separations from his sons. He wrote to them seldom, considering letters a woman's lot, but each Sunday he lit a candle for their well being, just in case their young age caused them to forget the prayers. That simple ritual seemed enough to tighten the knot between them and God. Then, on the way out of the chapel he would see their faces reflecting on the bottom of the cup filled with the holy water.

This falling out with Hugh was proving to be more burdensome than he had imagined. Each time thinking of his youngest son, he felt a stinging flow of blood to his cheeks. Strangely, anger was not the culprit. Brendan had inspected his own heart thoroughly, yet the only distinct sentiments he could identify were sorrow and perplexity.

Jostled inside the smoke-filled train car, Brendan leaned his forehead against the window and shut his eyes, trying to imagine Hugh in his new surroundings.

The young fool must be finished with work for the day. Did they at least pay him a fair wage? I bet they paid him less than they would another Brit. I bet they employed him just to save in wages. What possessed him to turn away from his real family? Those bloody Brits would never regard him as their equal! They may've opened their fake churches and lecture halls to him, but sure as hell not their hearts. Do they even have hearts? How long will it take for Hugh to see that he's not of their breed? No father wants to see his son deceived, used, mocked and cast off. I bet he'll come runnin' home again, like a battered cur. Mark my word, gents. Before the year is over, he'll be back in Tulsk. And you know what, gents? I'll take him and won't let him out again.

Back at home the smoke kept thickening. When Máirín learned what had happened at Carrick-on-Shannon, she did not weep or even say a word of reproach, which left Brendan scratching his head. He would have preferred to witness another scene of hysteria, complete with tears and strands of torn out hair. At least, that would have been something familiar to him. Instead, he felt lines of barbed wire stretching between him and his wife. Neither jokes nor kisses could tear down that fence. Máirín held her own maternal view of the situation. She cared nothing for the details of their quarrel. All she knew was that Brendan, a slave to his own crooked Fenian whims drove Hugh, her darling pet, away from home. Her mad husband had robbed her of a child, and that was beyond forgiveness.

Brendan kept reminding himself that Máirín understood nothing about patriotism and loyalty. How could she?

Typical woman! Selfish, earth-bound and oblivious to higher causes! No, she cannot see past her base Mama-bear instincts. Carryin', birthin', nursin' – all that she understands. Go on, woman, fill their bottomless bellies with meat pies and cider! But who shall fill their heads and hearts?

Still, Brendan did not want to see his wife in a state of perpetual grief. There is something extremely disturbing about witnessing women's and children's tears, no matter how firm a man's heart is. He always will always feel like a villain, even if he were in the right.

A few times Brendan tried to initiate a conversation with Máirín. Whenever he passed by her, he would brush the back of his hand against hers, as if accidentally, but each time she recoiled from his touch, shivering with disgust.

At night she lay with her face turned to the wall, stiff and silent, yet Brendan knew she was awake. He hated to admit the extent of his longing and frustration. This forced abstinence was becoming unendurable. It had never occurred to him to fear losing Máirín in this way. For over twenty years they slept in a carefree embrace, and now she avoided all intimacy with him.

Once he bought her a coral necklace, similar to the one she had seen at the Athlone Fair, and left it on her pillow in the morning just as she was about to awake. Máirín thanked him with a nod and put the necklace away in the drawer where it remained. The more Brendan tried to please his wife, the further she distanced herself from him.

There once was an ancient oak growing behind their house, their kissing tree. Against its wide mossy trunk, Brendan had pressed Máirín countless times. The giant protruding roots made for a comfortable bench, while the drooping branches cast enough shade, creating a leafy sanctuary. A week after Hugh's departure, the oak that had previously seemed like a monument to immortality suddenly started showing signs of rapid demise. Brown spots began appearing on the leaves, and the branches became fragile. The birds began abandoning their nests. Several dead hatchlings were found on the ground. It must have been some sort of parasitical disease, gnawing it from the inside. Máirín had arranged to have the tree cut down, lest it should fall and crush the roof of the house. One evening, when Brendan came home, he discovered a hole in the ground where the oak had once stood. Even the roots had been dug up and extracted. Brendan never learned how his wife managed to get rid of the tree in just one afternoon, whom she hired and how much money she paid. It must have taken at least five men to demolish this dying giant and to fully dispose of its corpse. Not a single branch was left, not a single acorn. A few times Brendan tried to fill the hole with soil, for some mysterious reason the freshly thrown soil kept receding, and the hole kept reappearing, growing deeper and steeper each time. Eventually, a crack ran across the plastered wall of the house. While pulling the roots out of the ground, the workers had damaged the foundation. Watching the crack spread and deepen, Máirín smiled bitterly. From a distance, it looked like an enormous spider had been weaving its web on the wall of the Malone house.

Burdened by the air of malice enveloping his cottage, Brendan avoided spending time there. This cracked clay box no longer felt like his home. He went inside only to change his clothes, eat or fetch some money. He spent his days in the fields and his nights in the barn.

On top of everything, the neighbors and the tenants were positively melting with curiosity to know what had become of Hugh and where he had vanished to after just a few days of staying at home, but Brendan had no strength left to deal with them. He simply left the truth at the mercy of their imaginations.

Not even once did he return to the Fenian camp after that humiliating evening. Right from the stables where he and Hugh finally had confronted each other, he had headed home, without facing his comrades for the fear of reading unanswerable questions in their eyes.

The only eyes into which Brendan could look without overwhelming unease were those of his eldest son. Dylan, for the simplicity and kindness of his nature, remained loyal to his father and sympathized with him sincerely. More than once he stopped at the threshold of the barn, Brendan's new home, and asked, "Dadaí, is there a thin' I can do?"

"No, lad. Why don't you go home to your wife? She must be waitin' for you."

"She can wait a bit longer. Listen, if you need help, let me know, and I'll do it."

"All right, I promise to call on you if somethin' comes 'round."

One time Dylan lingered at the door.

"Don't fret, Dadaí. We'll hear from him again. Say your prayers, and you'll make peace yet. He meant no offense, truly. Who knew it would turn out this way?"

Brendan would not mind reconciling with Hugh at all. That certainly would resolve a number of inconveniences. If anything, it would help him regain access to his marital bed, so he could stop feeling like a widower. Besides, reluctant as he was to admit it, Brendan pined for his youngest one with all his peculiarities. Of course, making the first step was unthinkable. Hugh would have to initiate the reconciliation. Brendan still considered his anger justified. Above all, he did not even have Hugh's address, and Belfast is no small city. In the meanwhile, Brendan could only hope that his son had not yet forgotten his old family and was not feeling too misplaced in his new one.

***

A sudden tap on the shoulder and a vaguely familiar voice knocked Brendan out of his reverie. Harry Daly, a former tenant, spotted him on the train.

"I'll be damned! Is that you, Mr. Malone?"

"It could be me, yes. How long has it been, Mr. Daly?"

"Four years. It feels like twenty, though. I never thought we'd meet again."

"I still can't believe you left for Derry. What the hell drove you there?"

"A good number of reasons," Harry replied energetically. "Village life simply isn't for me. I've known it long before my crops failed back in '04. I make a better official than an agrarian. At least, papers don't wither and rot before your eyes. But I marvel at the success of your youngest one. I was just on business in Belfast — "

Brendan's back suddenly became rigid.

"You saw Hugh?"

"Not in person. His photograph is in the newspaper. As a matter of fact, I have it here with me. Local bookworms edit it. I don't read such bosh, save for the commerce part, but this picture caught my eye. Here, take a look."

Brendan opened the newspaper hastily and recoiled, his eyes narrowed, as if from the sun. Right in the middle of the page he saw a totally unfamiliar young man in a dress suit, head all aglow from the pomade in his hair, thin lips stretched in a self-complacent grin beneath a charcoal mustache. Some elderly gentleman in a top hat and spectacles from a previous century was shaking his hand. *Professor Warwick welcomes the young University College graduate Hugh Malone into the top academic circle of Belfast"*, said the inscription under the photograph.

"So, is it truly your son, or do my eyes fool me?" Harry went on animatedly. "God, did he change! They praise his work here. I know nothing about such matters, but it sounds grand. But wait! Your name's also mentioned here."

124

"You're mockin', Mr. Daly!"

"May the good Lord strike dead me if I am! Read on, Mr. Malone."

Still squinting, Brendan recited half-audibly:

The young scholar was terse in the interview and merely said: "I wish to thank my father for making my education possible."

Harry snatched the paper from Brendan and folded it hastily, sensing that the photograph caused his former landlord considerable distress.

"You're one lucky devil, Mr. Malone, to have raised such a son! Even if some miracle happened and my lazy dimwitted Joe did achieve anything, you think he'd remember me for a second?"

"I can't vouch for your Joe," Brendan muttered, turning to the window.

***

Upon leaving the train station, Brendan got a disquieting impression that his acquaintances, all the folks whom he usually greeted with a reserved bow, were staring at him with a sort of pity and horror. And when he approached a small beer shop to buy a pitcher of ale, he heard Tom O'Neill whisper right behind his back. "How can Malone drink at time like this?"

"Perhaps, he doesn't know yet," Tom's wife suggested.

"How can he not know? Everyone knows! Such a stroke of misfortune... He'll have to sell his plot and flee."

The last thing Brendan needed at the moment was compassion from Tom of whom he never held a very high opinion.

"If it won't pain you, Mr. O'Neill", he began through his teeth, "would you mind tellin' me what the hell you're prattlin'?"

"He doesn't know!" Tom's wife squealed again, clinging to her husband's arm.

Brendan turned around, accidentally knocking off the beer pitcher with his elbow.

"What 'stroke of misfortune' do I have? True, those sons of dogs in Dublin tried to raise my property tax. But I went over and fixed the damned business, though it took me eight days. There, you've heard it all. Now, go home with God's grace! You caught me in bad humor."

The crowd doubled before Brendan could finish the phrase. Pale faces encircled him. Some already were already glistening with tears. The townspeople flocked around him, pressing tighter to each other, and watched, as one watches an execution. Then he saw Thaddeus McCluskey making his way through the crowd.

"Come with me," Thaddeus said lowly, seizing his neighbor by the arms and pulling him aside.

"For God's sake," Brendan muttered, glancing back at the half-empty beer glass, "explain what's happenin'. I'm losin' my wits."

"So am I, Brendan. Our lads are in trouble, grave as can be. They took it in their heads to raid the English headquarters. They shot three soldiers and wounded two. They had no time to escape. Do you know what charges were brought against them? Treason, conspiracy and murder! That's 'nough to have 'em both shot. Not a word was said in their defense. They're lost."

"Wait a minute now," Brendan said, blanching. "I'll be damned if I knew of whom you spoke just now. Who are *they*?"

"Don and Dylan! They led the whole thin'. There were other lads too, but they got away. Colin O'Nevin is terrified for his son Liam, but at least Liam broke free. 'Tis Don and Dylan now who'll pay with their lives."

And Thaddeus told the story to Brendan, as calmly as his emotional state permitted him, and as precisely as he knew it.

Just as Donnie had predicted, the trip to the river he and his mates had planned back in the beginning of the summer had worked miracles on their souls. Seven days of fishing and hunting, seven lukewarm nights of whiskey-gulping contests by the campfire, the surprise encounter with four Fenians who on their way from Carrick-on-Shannon to Athlone, made an adventurer's heaven. By the end of the week, however, Donnie felt quite ready to return to his wife.

"Wanderin' is good, but home-comin' is better yet!" he declared having spotted his cottage from a distance.

"'Tis true," Dylan confirmed. "Cozy beds and hot meals are callin' our names! Or could it be that we're agin' already?"

"What's to expect? Just think: I'm twenty-two and a father of three. Who wouldn't grow old? Those wenches, dimwitted as they are, surely got us tied up for keeps. God bless 'em!" Donnie laughed and speared his horse, screaming on the top of his throat, "Maggie! Maggie, darlin', I'm back!"

The smile vanished from his face the moment he saw his eldest son Timmy. The child was sitting on the porch alone, tangled in the folds of his sleeping shirt, tiny fist smudging dirt and tears across the swollen cheeks.

Donnie frowned when the boy, who would usually rush to him with a jubilant screech, did not react in any way to his arrival. And only when he picked Timmy in his arms, the child shook up and moved his bitten lips weakly.

"Mamaí…"

"Mamaí…what? She's well, I hope."

Donnie looked him in the eye inquisitively, forgetting that the child was not even three years old, and stepped inside the house.

Timmy stretched out his hand and pointed in the direction of the hay barn.

"Mamaí…" he repeated, and broke into quiet, helpless sobs.

Donnie handed his whimpering son over to Dylan and rushed inside the barn. At the door he suddenly froze and wavered. Right at his feet, lay a heap of crumbled clothes and tangled black hair which he recognized to be his wife. The sand beneath Maggie's head turned dark and sticky from the blood slowly dripping from the corner of her mouth and her nose. The slight trembling of her eyelids was the only evidence of life in her body. But Donnie, struck by the ashy color of her face, did not realize that at once and screamed.

Dylan's brain, softer and slower than that of an average man, was struggling to process what was happening before his eyes. Only three minutes ago everything was splendid. He and Donnie were on their way home, chatting and laughing.

As for little Timmy, at that stage of terror and confusion the boy could not even weep any longer. The sound of his father's scream sent him into stupor. Timmy closed his eyes and clung to Dylan's shoulder, assured that he was living his last moments. No doubt, the world was coming to an end since Dadaí was screaming like that.

Donnie shook his wife and then clasped her head to his chest, rocking from side to side. A slight tremor ran through Maggie's body, and a subtle hint of color returned to her cheeks. She coughed a few times, swallowing the blood.

"You gave me a fright," Donnie mumbled. "Good God… What happened here?"

She parted her swollen eyelids and gave him a dull stare without a hint of recognition. Then her head fell back again.

Having somehow managed to soothe the traumatized child, Dylan approached his brother-in-law and took him by the shoulders silently. Tears pooled in his corners of his eyes, for he was fond of Maggie. Earthy, patient and good-natured, she had been his undeclared sister for years, one of the few women he understood. Dylan's silent morning only lasted a moment. He lifted Maggie out of the arms of her husband, who still had not recovered from his shock, and carried her inside the house, muttering words of assurance. Little Timmy toddled after them mindlessly, while Donnie remained on the earthen floor, face in hands.

***

Dr. Shays, the only physician in Tulsk, was not at home when Dylan ran to fetch him. Mrs. Shays came in her husband's stead. Twenty years of assisting her husband had given her at least a basic knowledge necessary to stanch Maggie's bleeding and lessen her pain. Still, unlike her husband, Mrs. Shays had not quite mastered the ability to observe the patients' sufferings with detachment. While patching up the body of another woman who had been gruesomely violated, Mrs. Shays struggled to conceal her anger and disgust. She tried not to gasp, lest she should frighten the patient and her family members even more. A few times she turned away and covered her mouth with the sleeve of her blouse.

"My husband should return by tomorrow," said Mrs. Shays when her work was finished. "I shall send him to your house at once. If she gets worse, call me again."

As soon as the doctor's wife left, Donnie knelt by Maggie's bed and buried his face in the bend of her arm.

"I don't understand," he whispered. "I've only been gone for a week. In five years I've not been away for more than a day."

"One day is all it takes," Dylan replied under his breath, trying to rock Timmy to sleep. Suddenly, his eyes widened. "Christ, have mercy..." he whispered and tagged his brother-in-law by the collar. "Look, Don..."

Maggie's fist relaxed slowly, and right on the palm of her hand they saw a button from a British military uniform.

The Roscommon town policemen were in the habit of going to the villages on Fridays, claiming that the beer at the local pubs was better than even the one of the Guinness brewery in Dublin. On the way back, however, they behaved no better than those whom they would normally arrest in accordance to their duties. Quite often they would pass advances on young girls. But most of those girls came from impoverished families and usually put up no resistance, hoping that a quick surrender would earn them a shilling or two. Even their fathers and husbands, if they had any, condoned such barter. Donnie, on the other hand, was a landowner's son. Assured that Maggie, being his wife, was naturally outside of danger, he left her home alone without a second thought. He had not considered that the soldiers, after a few pitchers of beer, saw no difference between a desperate famished peasant girl and a landowner's wife. Roscommon women rarely manifest their wealth by wearing well-tailored clothes, and therefore look all the same to a drunken eye.

"I don't know which one did it," Donnie said in a changed voice and exhaled abruptly. "I'll just have to go and kill them all. That way I can't miss."

He leaped to his feet, but Dylan held him back by the elbow.

"Don, wait."

Donnie shoved him away.

"Shut your mouth, Dyl. There's not a damned thin' you can say to stop me."

"No, I wasn't thinkin' of stoppin' you. I meant I'll go with you."

"What for?" Donnie asked, shaking his head. "'Tis not your ordeal."

"Of course, 'tis my ordeal too, you bloody idiot!" Dylan shouted, seizing him again. "Very much mine… We're not strangers, are we? Besides, what can you do alone? We better call the lads."

"And who'll go with us? How many fools do you hope to find?"

"More than you think. And they're no fools."

***

Preparations diminish eagerness. Some things need to be done while anger is still fresh, while it overpowers all other feelings, while a flow of blood flushes fear from the heads. Without even discussing the strategy of the vengeance, Donnie's comrades grabbed their rifles off the walls.

In the hour that followed, Dylan learned what nobody ever taught him, not even his father. No fist fighting tournaments can prepare one for any resemblance of battlefield. In the pub one deals with adversaries, on the battlefield with enemies. Giving the neighbor a nosebleed, just to embrace him two minutes later, is not quite as aiming at somebody with the intention to end his life.

Overwhelmed by all the revelations, previously unimaginable, Dylan hardly paid attention to what was happening. He remembered neither the scream of his comrades attacking the garrison, nor the shooting. How did he manage to kill two British soldiers? He just fired without targeting, and the two men fell to the ground. A few bullets whistled next to his ear. Then everything in his head started spinning from a sudden pain in his right shoulder. The fall to the ground seemed to have lasted hours. In awe Dylan watched his hand release the rifle, the blood run down his palm in a multitude of intertwining lines and the moon above his head find refuge behind the clouds, as if refusing to play witness to the slaughter.

***

When Dylan opened his eyes he was surprised that his surrounding did not resemble Heaven where, according to his father's book of fairytales, all those who were killed in a battle congregated. He was lying on the floor of what appeared to be a prison cell. Those who had brought him there had not bothered to put him on one of the wooden bunk beds. For some time he simply stared before himself, without moving his head. The pain from the wound in the shoulder spread onto his entire right side, yet he suspected that his greatest pains lay ahead still. No, it certainly was not Heaven.

So, I'm still alive, he thought without any particular emotion. But how much longer?

Then he heard the squeaking of a key opening a rusty lock and saw a pair of muddy boots right before his face.

"On your feet, chieftain!"

The last word had an exhilarating effect on Dylan; his father called him thus. So, he was an official hero! Even the enemies could not deny that.

"Get up! We're going to see the captain."

And the soldier jerked Dylan up by the wounded arm, as if trying to tear it out of the joint.

Dylan clenched his teeth and pulled himself up. For a second he felt dizzy, but then the pain and the weakness retreated into the background. He made a firm decision to behave as audaciously as his temper would allow. He tossed head back and measured the soldier the most defiant, mocking glance he could produce at that moment. Without a word, he let the guards handcuff and drag him out of his cell.

Walking down the corridor, he saw his friend. Donnie's hands also were tied behind his back, and his shirt also was stained with blood, but his face bore an expression far less defiant. The two managed to establish a brief eye contact, and Dylan winked. But the guard noticed that and shoved him in the back.

"Walk!"

A few minutes later Dylan was standing before the police captain himself.

"Dylan Malone?"

"That's what my university diploma says," a smug reply followed.

The captain's mouth twitched incredulously.

"*You* went to a university?"

"Why yes, sir! Three years of superior education, at University College Dublin of all places. I recommend it highly!"

Dylan spoke without any thoughts or fears, just like he did when he was drunk.

"Fancy that!" said the captain, tapping his desk with a pencil. "Courage, sharp wit, scholastic achievements… Your father must be proud of you. What a grief it must be to lose such a son. You know what's in store for you, don't you?"

Dylan shook his head innocently.

"No, sir, not yet. But I can't wait to find out."

"Well, then it's my duty to inform you, Malone. I'll be brief. No later than two days from now you'll be tried for treason, conspiracy and murder."

The captain articulated the last words, leaving generous pauses between them.

"Is that all?" Dylan asked, bobbing his disheveled head.

"Why, it doesn't sound grave enough for you?"

"Much too grave, sir! All we did was play with some rifles. If you could only explain my crime to me—"

The captain dropped the pencil and addressed the guard:

"Howard, take him to Felton. He'll talk to him the proper way. I've no time to waste on this nonsense."

Dylan beamed again. His victory cost him but a few rude, not particularly clever remarks.

The next thing he remembered was a blindfold covering his eyes and Howard's cold hand leading him down an endless stairwell. So, that was the British way of dealing with crime, taking their captives on the tour from one room to another. They make a ceremony of it, with all those arrests, questionings and trials. So many words, spoken and written; anything to overshadow the truth!

Howard's hands dragged Dylan into a hot, humid room in the basement and then pushed him into an unpadded chair. The prisoner's eyes remained covered with a dark rag.

"Well, gentlemen," Dylan spoke, in the same tone, "if you still want to have a heartfelt talk with me, let me at least see your faces."

This time nobody replied to his remark.

"The captain told me to bring him here," the guard told Felton. "He's not just one of the attackers. He's also an IRB member."

"Another one?" a grim voice queried. "By God, Howard, how many of them are there?"

"Apparently, more than we had surmised. This is no ordinary revenge skirmish. This incident shall be reported directly to Dublin Castle. Ah, the lovely facts that surface! You think you've caught a simple sparrow in your net, and then you discover he has a belly full of gunpowder."

"Imagine! This Fenian comedy must be in fashion again. It all started after Clarke's return. I swear, every time one of them returns from America, there's a massive flare-up of patriotism. In God's name, how many of them are there?"

"Thus far we have only four in custody. This strapping hero standing before you is the one who killed Blake and Dalton. The rest is up to you to find out."

"The first one was mute. What was his name? McCluskey! I couldn't get a word out of him. He must've pinned his tongue to his cheek."

"You'll just have to try with this one," said Howard. "Dazzle me with your investigative efforts. Felton, you're the master! We need answers."

"What sort of answers?" Dylan asked. "I have no secrets. What is it that you want to know, gentlemen? Where my Dadaí had buried his treasure chest?"

Before he could finish the phrase, his teeth collided with the floor. Felton, unlike his comrades, did not believe in unnecessary ceremonies. Not that he completely hated his work. No, he even found certain pleasure in observing those who went through his hands, but he wanted it done properly. The previous victim turned out somewhat stubborn, and Felton needed to uphold his reputation as Master Inquisitor. Another failure would put his skill in question.

Unable to see his tormentor, Dylan could not believe that Felton had only two feet and two fists. There was no way to escape the blows, no place to crawl away to and catch his breath, because they would find him anywhere. Dylan could only thank God for the numbness that was rapidly spreading over his body. After a while he no longer needed to clench his teeth to keep himself from moaning. Only one time he shuddered, when Felton poured whiskey on the open wound in his shoulder.

"It's only whiskey, the cure for all illnesses! And you call yourself Irish! Does this hurt? Be easy, soon you'll be the chieftain again. In hell!"

Those were the last words Dylan heard that day. He did not know for how long Felton continued thrashing him after he had lost consciousness for the second time.

Dylan's second awakening was slow, uneasy and incomplete. He perceived a wrinkled face bowed over him, felt cold, dry fingers on his wrist and heard a droning voice:

"He's had his fill for now. A bit too much dedication on your part, Felton. He needs to stand before the judge. Be mindful of that with your next victim. The lads need to look presentable for the execution."

Marveling at the endurance of his feet that still were able to hold him up, Dylan arrived at the courtroom, convoyed by Howard. Donnie was sitting just two yards away but he had no strength to raise his eyes on his friend. Not that they needed any words or looks. Over the past few days their lives were like two shores of the same river - a bit closer to each other at times, or farther apart, but inevitably destined for the same end.

With a strange indifference they listened to the accusations brought up against them. Even the death sentence seemingly made no impression on either one. Shortage of money, sickness, falling out with mates, ill-timed love; those calamities can strike a twenty-two year old as realistic, but not death.

"'Tis but a bad dream," Dylan whispered.

"Right you are." Donnie nodded. "But who shall 'waken us?"

A second later, a woman's voice resounded from the end of the hall, "Let me see my husband!"

Pushing away the guards who were trying to hold her back, Maggie broke into the courtroom. Barefoot, her hair loose, her face black with bruises, bulging eyes with dilated pupils, she resembled a witch. After regaining her senses and learning the news of her husband's arrest, she found enough strength to run to him.

Donnie did not turn around but only shrank and hung his head even lower. Maggie's shrieks dragged him back to reality. Now he knew for certain that it was not a dream. Death herself was clinging to his shoulders with the stiff, icy fingers of his wife. If his hands were free, he would have covered his ears to save himself from that banshee's cry. Donnie feared that he would scream too if she stayed with him for another second. How was he supposed to maintain composure now? No, Maggie would not let him go with dignity. There are good reasons why women are not allowed on ships or in war camps. They should not be allowed inside courtrooms either.

The guards managed to pry Maggie's hands off Donnie's shoulders, finger by finger, and drag her out into the hall.

Dylan, who witnessed that stomach-churning scene of female hysteria, thought that if Caitlin had been there, she would have probably behaved in the same manner, and he would not have survived it. Maggie's squealing had already done enough to undermine his stoicism. A woman's tears mean to liquefy a man's will.

Blessedly, Caitlin never came. Having spent the last three weeks in bed, she would not risk endangering her unborn baby, not even to lift her husband's spirit in his last hours. The pains of pregnancy had made Caitlin indifferent to the sufferings of others.

Maybe the truth is bein' kept from her, Dylan thought. That's it! She must still believe I'm huntin' 'long the shores of the Shannon, accompanied by my mates. Whatever you've been told 'bout your husband, Catlin, stay where you are. No good will come out of you seein' me or me seein' you.

***

Lying on the wooden bench of his cell the night before his execution, Dylan took the opportunity to reflect on the twenty-two years that he had lived and on the ten hours that remained. His mind had never been more lucid than in those last hours, as he was staring into the empty eye-sockets of Death. He almost wanted

Felton to beat him again and empty his head. Suddenly, Dylan noticed that all his thoughts were directed at one blasphemously simple question that he had never dared ask before.

What in Heaven's name am I sufferin' for? All that blood sacrifice... *What good shall come out of it? Is this what every man thinks the night* *before his execution?*

How Dylan wished he could invoke the spirits of the Manchester Martyrs, whose deaths he had exulted in a song on Frankfurt Avenue in 1908. No doubt, his performance had amused the three rebel spirits. If only they would deign to come down to him! No, he would not trouble them with frivolous inquiries about the afterlife. He had but one question for them: would they still have sacrificed their lives for the same cause again?

Then his thoughts turned to Wolf Tone, the leader of the United Irishmen, who slashed his own throat to cheat the hangman after the judge had refused him a death by a firing squad. The proud rebel died on his own terms from his own hand. Dylan would have gladly followed Wolf Tone's example, but he did not have any sharp objects within his reach. His captors had seen to it. All his belongings had been confiscated from him, including the penknife, a present from Dadaí. Even the cross that had a sharp tip had been pulled from his neck. Dylan's only way to escape the execution was to smash his head against the wall, but that would require strength that he no longer possessed.

It was his first real temptation. He started praying, but every time his thoughts turned to his father. The God he envisioned had Brendan's face. The two authoritative patriarchal images blended in one. Dylan hardly knew whom exactly he addressed as "Father" in his silent, disconnected monologue.

Where are you now? For twenty-two years I've listened to you, my *mouth agape. I already know by heart your speeches on loyalty and* *patriotism. But tell me now: am I a hero or a fool? There's not a whole* *bone left in my body. Will my knuckles be restored in the next life? Or was my brother right to wash his hands and run away? I don't expect you to save me. Just tell me that I'm not dyin' in vain. Tell me that I was more than just a lure for the enemy. Scatter my doubts, and I'll die content. One look, one word from you, and I'll believe you.*

The guards at the entrance to the prison turned out to be surprisingly humane. They rarely communicated with Felton or Howard. The atrocities that took place in the basement remained a mystery to them. Calmly, almost reverently, they escorted Brendan to his son's cell. Usually such closeness between the prisoners and their visitors was not easily permitted, unless a death sentence was involved.

When Brendan saw his eldest son, the iron bars of the cell tripled in his eyes, and he had to grasp them in order to prevent himself from falling. Dylan's head was hanging off the edge of the wooden bench so low that his face could not be seen through the hair. Still, the most horrifying sight was his arm in the torn blood stained sleeve, with shattered knuckles and discolored nails. For a few seconds, everything in Brendan' view appeared like looking through a crimson glass.

"Son, what have they done to you?" he whispered.

His voice roused Dylan. His neck vibrating with tension, the boy lifted his head to look up at his father.

When their eyes met, another wave of vertigo came over Brendan. That dark, shapeless mask could not be his son's face. There was nothing familiar in it, neither the features nor the expression.

Only a week ago, before Brendan's departure for Dublin, they went out on horseback together. It was a short expedition without a definite destination or any practical purpose, an opportunity for a father and his son to ride nowhere and talk about nothing, changing topics on a whim or simply keeping silence. How confidently Dylan's hands gripped the reigns. How his copper hair fluttered in the wind over his strong neck. He rode, throwing glances over his shoulder now and then, the child of Brendan's dreams, the only blessing in his life that came without a hidden trick, the only gold coin that shone on both sides. And now, what was he turned into? A twitching lump of swollen flesh and broken bones...

The guard unlocked the door.

"Fifteen minutes, Mr. Malone."

"Dadaí!" Dylan called out rushing towards the bars, but after the first steps his knees bent, and he sprawled on the floor. "Why are you standin' here? Why don't you come in, Dadaí?"

He stretched his hand forward, like a hungry man begging for bread, but the remains of his strength gave away and he collapsed with a spasmodic sigh, his eyes widely open and fixed on the space between bars.

Brendan slowly subsided on the floor next to Dylan and rested his hand on his son's forehead, feeling how sticky his hair was with blood and sweat.

"I'm here."

Then Dylan started speaking, hastily, as if fearing to swoon before finishing the phrase or to forget something.

"'Tis good you came, Dadaí. I confess I was afraid earlier today. Thoughts passed through my head, rotten thoughts. I'm even shamed to tell you what they were... But they're gone now. See? I'm at ease. I feel no pain. My body's dead already. So, why should I fear the execution? You know why I'm here, don't you? Rest easy, Dadaí, I told them nothin', not a word. I've kept to the Oath. The words are still fresh in my head. Aren't you pleased?"

He paused for a moment to take a breath and to hear the desired response, but Brendan remained silent.

"Dadaí? Answer me," Dylan entreated, sinking what was left of his nails into his father's knee. "'Tis what you've always wanted of me, right? Well, say somethin'. One bloody word…"

Brendan took his son's discolored face in his hands and tilted it up.

"Yes, chieftain. Of course, 'tis the very thin' I wanted of you."

What else could he say?

"You couldn't have done a better deed for your people," he added in a second. "And be sure, they won't forget it. You've made Dadaí proud."

Dylan's crusted lips stretched. The tiny wounds reopened and began to bleed.

"Tell me one last thin', Dadaí. Will I still go to Heaven, even though I killed two men, and the church says 'tis wrong to kill? Remember what Father O'Malley said?"

"Enemies don't count," Brendan declared with unflinching conviction.

"They don't? But the church also teaches to love your enemy and turn the other cheek."

"We've been turnin' the other cheek for seven centuries."

"No, we haven't, Dadaí. Weren't there revolts b'fore us?"

"Those weren't true revolts though. I don't know, son… Just don't let that unsettle your soul. You'll surely go to Heaven. And if you don't, that will only mean that Heaven doesn't exist. And that's not what Father O'Malley would teach."

Brendan could not think up anything more convincing at that moment, hardly even conscious of his own words. A random thought zoomed through his head:

"Dear God, please let me trade places with my child. Let him out. Let him walk the earth for a bit longer. If he dies, how shall *I* live?"

"Dadaí," Dylan went on. "I want you to do one thin'. Find Hugh, make peace with him. Soon he'll be your only son. Be kind to him. He's taken so much unkindness already. Don't mock him if his nose bleeds. 'Tis my last wish."

Brendan promised he would do so. Immediately, something within him altered, as if his heart dressed in armor. It was not the time to grieve. The pain froze and retrieved into the remote corner of his consciousness. There it would stay until the due moment when it finally could be released and felt thoroughly.

"I promise, chieftain," Brendan repeated, in a firmer tone. "I'll find him, even if I must search the whole of Northern Ireland."

The door of the cell creaked.

"Your time's up, Mr. Malone!"

"Go, Dadaí," Dylan whispered and pushed his father's hands away. "Mamaí needs you. Tell her not to weep for long. I need no mournin' masses. Tell Caitlin she can marry whomever she wants to after I'm gone. I don't want her to be alone with a baby. That would be a rotten station. Go now."

***

When Brendan walked out of the prison building, he did not notice the changes that had occurred in the sky, neither the twilight nor the rain. He walked all through the night, and towards the dawn, his feet somehow brought him back to the village. There, he saw a procession slowly moving towards the cemetery. Without saying a word, Brendan joined at the very end, staring downwards at the hundreds of footprints in the mud, listening to the dull creaking of the funeral carriage.

Again, he noticed that people were giving him same looks as just a few hours ago at the train station. He did not think much of it and kept walking after the coffin. It must have been someone else's tragedy. He had his own to deal with his own. He hardly even recognized the faces of his neighbors and his tenants.

Then somebody took him by the arm, lead him to the first row. He followed unconsciously. When Brendan's daughter-in-law, who by then was in the eighth month of pregnancy, buried her face in his chest and burst into sobs, his face expressed a mild wonder. He could not even muster the strength to lift his arms and return the embrace. He simply stared down into the crown of Caitlin's disheveled head as if he had never seen her before.

"Who's that?" some adolescent boy asked, pointing at Brendan.

"'Tis Mr. Malone, our landlord," a reluctant reply followed. "His wife killed h'self, slashed her wrists. The neighbors found her on the floor in a pool o'blood. Her eldest son was just sentenced to death. The priest was hard set 'gainst buryin' her on the church ground. We had to implore him, all of us."

In twenty-one year of his life Hugh had become acquainted with various forms of grief, superficially with some, a bit deeper with others, but oddly enough, bereavement had never been the cause of it. Tragedies would loom by, often two inches from his skin, but never quite touching him. More than once he witnessed a widow, old or young, crumble over her husband's grave, the black cloth of her dress enhancing the pallor of her face. He watched tiny coffins carried to the graveyard, heard the laments of the mother dragging after them like a somber veil.

Hugh was endowed with enough compassion to commiserate with others but not the courage to envision himself in their place. He comforted himself thinking that in the nearest future, no losses were in store for his family. His parents were still fairly young. Brendan could still defeat Dylan in fist fighting, and Máirín had not given up her dream of giving birth to a daughter, so she would not have to be the only female in the house. And least of all could Hugh imagine his merry, spunky brother lowered into the ground.

It was no wonder that the news of what had happened in Roscommon reached Belfast only a week after the executions. The local authorities, anxiety-bound, kept the word from spreading beyond the border of the county, lest the rest of the Irish population should become infected with sympathy towards the rebels. The last thing Ireland needed was another crop of Manchester Martyrs.

When Hugh learned about Dylan's death he pressed his fists to his chest and whispered, "All along I've feared it was coming. My life's been going much too smoothly as of late, it was beginning to unsettle me. The sorrow in my life has been renewed. Dylan and Mamaí at once..."

He averted his eyes from his family, remembering that the reckless act that brought his brother to death was directed against the English. For Hugh's sake, the Ashleys had tacitly allied not to mention the circumstances around Dylan's execution. Even John abandoned his usual sarcasm and embraced his brother-in-law.

"I suppose, it doesn't sound particularly credible coming from me," he said, "but Dylan wasn't that terrible of a fellow. He certainly held to his principles, however absurd they may have been."

"He was a tremendous fellow," Hugh replied, shaking his head. "I knew him like no one else did, not even Dadaí. Dylan had the gentlest of hearts. War simply wasn't in his blood. All he wanted was an ordinary, peaceful life, and he had a thousand reasons to live. Now he won't even see his own child. And Mamaí—I didn't write her a single letter over the summer."

Agitated by his own words, Hugh tossed from one corner of the living-room into another, until he finally froze by the window, eyes shut, hands clasped behind his back.

"Poor Dadaí," he whispered. "I pity him more than I would anyone else. Please, God, help me find the proper words to console him, at least temporarily. He had harbored such hopes for Dylan! I must return to Roscommon."

Edith stood up hastily and declared that she was going with him.

"No, you absolutely can't!" Hugh sounded almost frightened. "It's not the safest place right now."

"And that is precisely why I can't allow you to go alone. Your desire to be with your parents, and I desire to be with you—if my wishes count for anything. If I stay here, I shall go mad worrying."

Professor Ashley took his daughter by the arm and pulled her aside.

"Edith, it pains me to say this, but I must agree with your husband. I do not think that you should go."

She responded with nervous, hostile laughter.

"Of course, there's a drunken IRB member with a rifle sitting behind every bush, just waiting to shoot me!"

"The physical danger is not the only reason," the professor continued with the insinuating softness of a physician tending to an ill child. "I honestly doubt that now would be the most appropriate time for you to meet Mr. Malone, even if to express your condolences."

"There never will be an appropriate time, Papa!" Edith exclaimed defiantly, freeing her arm. "Two months, two years from now I will still be English, and his firstborn will still be dead. I was hoping that at a time like this trifle of this sort wouldn't matter."

The Professor nodded weakly.

"Now is not the time to demand that of your father-in-law to step over his prejudices. It's my paternal intuition, and you'll simply have to trust it, dear girl. I don't expect you to understand fully what is happening in Mr. Malone's heart right now, but I expect you to trust my judgment and respect my wishes."

"Respect your wishes…" Edith whispered aside and let out a bitter chuckle. "Paternal intuition! This must be a new term in psychology. It's but a complicated way of saying: 'Papa knows best!' How can I possibly counter that?"

Professor Ashley was more than eager to absorb his daughter's anger. No, he did not mind it in the least. It would be better if she yelled at her father than at her husband. Hugh needed to be sheltered from additional hostility.

"Dear girl, you have a long life ahead, God willing," the professor continued. "You will have numerous opportunities to meet your new Irish family under more favorable circumstances. I am certain that at the present moment, Hugh and his father will have a better understanding of each other if left alone. Believe me, you're not one of the people Mr. Malone wishes or needs to see in the immediate future."

Edith swept her hand over her forehead and stood silently for a few seconds.

"All right, I shall remain here," she said at last, not exactly obeying but rather surrendering with a grudge. "You two have united against me. I am outnumbered. In certain civilized countries, this is called democracy. Consider that you have won by popular vote. Hugh, take your time to settle your family matters and return whenever you are ready. But do me a favor. Return without any holes in your body. I'm not sure if I could patch them up."

"Nothing will happen to me," Hugh attempted to reassure her, aware of how unconvincingly he sounded. "I shall return as soon as the situation becomes... acceptable."

Sensing that his words did not have the desired effect on his wife, he turned away from the window and attempted to embrace her, but Edith pushed his hands away, her resentment still raw.

"Let her fume," the professor whispered to Hugh. "See that you do not adopt the habit of appeasing your wife or apologizing to her every time she pouts. Remember, you are not obliged to justify your every single action to her. A willful girl like my daughter will forget her place very quickly if you allow her to ask too many questions. Edith will take advantage of your willingness to accommodate her whims. It would pain me to see you, a gentleman that you are, trampled down by her. You are allowed to see your family without her tagging along."

Edith knew that her father was trying to impart some manly wisdom to her husband behind her back, even though she could not make out the exact words. Clearly, they did not care that she could still hear bits of the conversation. They had not bothered waiting until she was completely out of sight. Being older than her husband and having a comparable income did not necessarily translate into having the final say. On the contrary, the realization of his junior status would motivate Hugh to fight all the harder to assert his masculine superiority in their marriage. Their egalitarian honeymoon could not last forever. Professor Ashley made it quite clear in regards to whose side he favored. He would not allow his daughter to nag and manipulate her husband whose resistance had been weakened under duress. The professor was willing to condone an impressive number of petty transgressions, including premarital encounters in the shady guestroom, but not female tyranny.

Suddenly, an idea occurred to Edith, an idea so clever that the men in her family would not dare to dismiss it. A distant relative of theirs had served in the army and after retiring, left his uniform to the professor as a keepsake. The uniform had been stored in the attic along with the rest of relics, including late Mrs. Ashley's furs and gowns.

Beaming at her ingenuity, Edith retrieved the uniform, carried it into the living-room and shook it out in front of everyone, raising a cloud of dust.

"I hear they check everyone's papers in Roscommon," she said, handing the coat to her husband, still avoiding eye contact with him. "They might suspect you in taking part in the attack. After all, you are Dylan's brother. What could you say in your defense? But if you dress like one of them, perhaps they won't bother you. If you won't let me accompany you, will you at least take this uniform? I still won't sleep at night, but perhaps, I won't toss and turn as much."

"There is a simpler, more traditional solution that does not involve costumes and props," the professor said. "I could obtain a letter from the constabulary testifying to your character and your disassociation from the IRB. You are a respectable young scholar, and my colleagues will confirm that."

"Getting a piece of paper signed and stamped can take days." Hugh shook his head. "The constable has more pressing matters than writing recommendation letters. No, I must leave today. Besides, do you really wish to draw the authorities' attention to the fact that your son-in-law has relatives in the IRB? Is that something you wish to carry with you everywhere? No matter what your colleagues say in my defense, the Ashleys will not shed sunshine on the Malones. Quite the opposite. The Malones shall cast a shadow on the Ashleys. I do not want suspicion hanging over this house. One murmur is enough to undermine the reputation of an entire family. It takes one second to taint one's name and many years to clear it. It only takes a drop of poison to ruin a glass of wine. And please, do not say anything to Mr. Clayton either. If he asks, just tell him I had a death in the family. This idea with the uniform is so wild that I'm actually willing to consider it."

Swiftly, he slipped out of his morning jacket and put on the military coat, reminiscing of the New Year's masquerade back at University College and the Turkish costume he wore that night. This game of disguise could be almost thrilling, had the circumstances been less tragic. The uniform fit well, apart from being a bit wide in the shoulders. Hugh span around with his arms elevated, still adjusting to the feeling of stiff wool.

"I can imagine my father's face when he sees me," he said, smirking grimly. "Dadaí will put a bullet in my head before I have a chance to explain him everything. Am I forgetting something? I just know that there's something of importance that keeps eluding me. Ah, I'll probably remember it when I'm on the train. Keep me in your prayers. And tell Jerry Clayton to study his Latin. I expect him to have his lesson learned by the time I return."

***

On his way to Roscommon, Hugh lost his perception of time entirely. How long did he wait for the train in the night? How long did he ride, listening of the monotonous rattle of the wheels? Two hours? Five?

A few of the passengers who shared his train car wore the same British uniforms. They stared at him steadfastly and quizzically. They must have expected him to greet them or at least nod his head. Usually, soldiers and policemen acknowledge each other's presence, even if they are not inclined to start a conversation.

Hugh was not keeping any notice of his surrounding, as his thoughts were fixed wholly on the upcoming reunion with his parents. He kept wondering how Brendan would receive him and what they would have to say to one another. Somehow, he would have to cross the threshold of his native house.

In the breast pocket of Hugh's military jacket there was a letter that Edith had written to Brendan. She slipped the envelope to him at the last moment as they were kissing each other goodbye at the train station. Hugh was not sure if he had the right to familiarize himself with the content of the letter. Should he just give it to his father without reading? And what would be the most appropriate time? After an hour of agonizing, Hugh finally opened the envelope. The length of the note provided him with instant relief. His secret fear was to discover an enormous tome filled with bitterness, pathos and sentimentality. He was looking at a plain white piece of paper with just a few lines written in clean handwriting.

Dear Mr. Malone
I regret not being able to express my condolences in person. Please know that our grief for Dylan and Mrs. Malone is as sincere and profound as our love for Hugh. Do not feel obliged to respond to this letter. Even if

*you decide that you and I should never meet, please know that I am proud
to wear your family surname. May the Almighty protect you!*
   --Edith Malone

Hugh could not have composed anything so dignified and
laconic. Edith would make a fine diplomat. She had managed to
say what needed to be said in less than a hundred words. Reading
his wife's message made Hugh a little less apprehensive about the
upcoming reunion with his father. If Edith, who had never met
Brendan, could find the courage to write to him, then his own son
should have the courage to hand the letter over to him. Only a few
minutes ago Hugh was praying for the train to break down, so he
could delay the dreaded encounter by another few hours, and now
he could not wait for the conductor to announce his station. He
spent the rest of the ride on his feet in the vestibule of the car. He
was too late for Dylan and Máirín, but he would not be late for
Brendan.

*I'm coming, Dadaí. Another hour or two, and we shall embrace. You
and Caitlin and her child – that's all that's left of the Malones in Tulsk.*

Then he was dashing against the wind, hardly feeling any
ground beneath his feet.

Since his early childhood Hugh had been identifying his house
in the twilight by the shape of the windows glowing with that pale-
orange light that no other house seemed to exude. Each time he
would see his mother's frail silhouette against the background of
that light, as she was waiting for her sons to come home. As soon
as Hugh would cross the threshold, all reproaches for staying out
too late would fly out of her head instantly. Máirín would free the
boys of their stiff autumn jackets and herd them towards the
dinner table. Her hair and the entire room smelled like sunflowers
all year long.

There's nobody waiting for me there, thought Hugh. No
wonder there are no lights in the windows.

After a few seconds of hesitation, he licked his parched lips and he rapped on the door with his knuckles. If he knocked too loudly, it would startle his father and make him think that the police had come to arrest him. At the same time, he needed to be heard. No sound came from within. No motion could be detected.

He must be asleep, he attempted to reason with himself and knocked a bit bolder, still not daring to call out for them.

Again, no response came. Hugh sighed and jerked the handle a few times.

Wake up, Dadaí. It's your other son, the black sheep. Let me in.

A wave of subconscious, unexplainable terror, like that of a sleeping man when a snake crawls by, engulfed him.

To his astonishment, Hugh discovered that his moist, trembling hands kept stubbornly sliding off the door handle. This was the house where his mother had killed herself. He could almost smell her blood in the air. He suddenly wanted to run away from the place.

What's happening to me?

And the same second a bullet pierced his back right between the shoulder blades.

Hugh did not even hear the shot. All of his senses switched off immediately. It seemed that Death had been waiting for him there for quite a while. And when he collapsed onto the steps of his own house it hastily fetched his soul, like a swift hound fetches a prey killed an instant ago by the hunter.

Brendan lowered his rifle and, without throwing another glance at his house, dove back into the forest. Over the past two weeks he had forgotten that he still had a body that required nourishment and rest. Though hungry, he could not eat. Though exhausted, he could not sleep. He drank relentlessly. There was enough whiskey and beer in his cellar to last a whole year, but eventually even the alcohol stopped working. Brendan could no longer slip into that foggy numbness called intoxication. He spent a few days outside the empty house, staring at the spreading crack on the wall. He would not have minded for the clay box to crumble before his eyes. If anything, it would add a touch of finality to that chapter of his life, making it that much easier for him to leave the village for good. But the house never crumbled. It continued standing as a monument to Brendan's failures as husband, father and landlord. The only role in which he could still prove and redeem himself was that of a patriot. He was excused from all obligations save for those before his country. This sudden realization of his moral freedom made the killing of the young British soldier appear so natural. From that moment on, that became Brendan's sole obligation — to shoot all those who wore the uniform. If he saw the familiar dark-blue coat, he would apply every effort to make a hole in it, preferably in the area of the breast, where the medals usually were displayed.

There in the twilight he collided face to face with Colin O'Nevin whose emotional state seemed to have stabilized. Two days earlier, Colin finally reunited with his sons who managed to escape from the police on the night of the attack on the British garrison. One of the boys crawled to his house after dark, miraculously avoiding the night patrol, just to inform his father about their well being. No longer having any reasons for despair, Colin fell under the impression that nothing in this universe towered above his shoulder. Following his cherished habit, he plunged boldly into everyone else's affairs.

"You've got a queer look on your face," he addressed Brendan. "What've you done?"

"I killed him," a nonchalant response followed.

"Killed whom?"

"The bloody soldier! He was pacin' round my house, so I shot him down. I bet the scum was thinkin' how to get inside, fill his pockets with trinkets. You know they disdain nothin'."

"How did you know 'twas a Brit?"

"He wore a British uniform, you idiot! Anyone who dresses thus deserves a bullet in his back. 'Tis a memorial mass for Dylan."

"So, what happens now?"

"Only God knows, O'Nevin. My job's done here. Why would I stick 'round if I've got nothin' to do? I'm headin' towards Carrick."

"I was thinkin' the same," Colin spoke animatedly, reinforcing his words by frantic gestures. "I never gave the Oath. Not for lack of desire, mind you. The state of family affairs simply wouldn't allow. Still, I've got friends 'mong the Fenians. They ought to give my boys shelter, wouldn't you think?"

When Colin mentioned his sons, Brendan frowned. The Fenian camp was not meant as a shelter for fugitives who were not members. Protecting every restless soul that had a falling out with the law was not the primary function of the Brotherhood. However, this time around the circumstances were out of the ordinary. After all, Colin's sons broke the law and endangered themselves to avenge a violated Irishwoman, and that could pass for an informal pledge.

"I'll talk to Aidan if need be," Brendan replied sternly and impatiently. "He won't turn you and your lads down, not after everythin' they've done. But listen, O'Nevin, be a lamb and don't say a bloody word."

"To whom? 'Bout what?"

"I meant, shut the hell up, O'Nevin! At least, until the mornin', will you? I feel rotten. I can't talk now."

"All right, then…" Colin resigned with a mock bow. "High and mighty, are we? I'll be mute as a fish."

About a quarter of a mile deeper into the woods Colin's three sons, Liam, Doug and Matt were waiting with their horses ready.

"Is the road clear?" Colin asked them.

"Yes, Dadaí. 'Tis safe to go."

***

In a few hours they reached Carrick-on-Shannon. Even from a distance, Brendan noticed that something odd was happening in the camp. There was not a trace of usual festivity. The Fenians, tense and bewildered, congregated in small groups around withering campfires. They interacted with one another in sighs, tentative glances and unfinished phrases. It seemed that nobody permitted himself to sit down or even light a pipe.

Brendan spurred up his horse, causing his companions to fall behind. Basil Costello was the first one who spotted him.

"Where've yer been all this time?" the old man asked. "We thought yer dead, or worse. Haven't yer heard wha' happened? They've got Aidan."

"How in devil's name could that happen?" Brendan asked, dismounting.

Obeying the force of habit, he shook Basil's cold trembling hand and surveyed the camp, as if still hoping to see Aidan's face in the crowd.

"Nobody's sure yet how it happened," the old man continued. "First he went off to Dublin on some business and never came back. We waited for him and waited some more. Then, two weeks later we get the news that he's in prison!"

Brendan glanced at the log cabin where Aidan had lived for months on end. Any second the door would open, and the chieftain would emerge. No light was shining from the window, but that did not mean anything, because Aidan had always kept his cabin dark. Ever since his head injury in South Africa, his eyes had been intolerant to candlelight. Even staring at a campfire from a distance could provoke an attack of agonizing headache. It was not unusual for Aidan to conduct his initiation meetings in the dark. He jokingly referred to himself as *Fear Dorcha*, the Dark Man, which had also been the nickname of Matthew O'Neill, the Baron of Dungannon and the father of the legendary Red Hugh. Aidan had no qualms about comparing himself to great historical figures. One could certainly not accuse him of modesty. But where was he now?

"Who brought the news?" Brendan asked when he finally accepted the fact that Aidan's cabin really was empty.

"She did."

Basil pointed his knobby finger at the woman who was conversing with one of the Fenians. She was wearing a coarse woolen cape with a hood that concealed her hair.

"Isabel?" Brendan asked, narrowing his eyes.

When the woman turned around, he noticed that she was already in her forties, although from the back she could have easily been mistaken for someone half her age, so slight was her frame. Her movements communicated a sort of willful immediacy.

"I am Isabel's mother," she replied

Brendan trembled in reverence. Right in front of him stood Countess Markiewicz, the Fenian queen, one of the few women before whom he would actually consider kneeling.

"My lady..." he stammered, placing one hand on his heart and stretching another forward.

"Please call me Constance," she corrected him immediately and categorically. "Aidan and his men have always addressed me in this manner. My surnames and titles have changed over the years, but my given name remains the same. And what is your name? I don't recall meeting you."

Brendan did not respond at once. For years this woman had been his demi-deity that he praised aloud at every opportunity, but never dreamed of encountering in person, and least of all here, on the cold shores of Shannon, amidst his comrades. Her image had always remained a radiant obscurity to him. She bore a nobility title and a foreign surname. The popular fables surrounding her were worthy of an epic by Yeats.

***

Constance Markiewicz was one of those rare women whose inner fire burns brightly enough to melt the bars of the golden cage. Not always sure what she wanted from life, she always knew exactly what life wanted from her. Every act was a step towards the goal set for her by God; therefore, she had no habit of repenting. No public condemnation, no malice could distract her from her mission or poison her benevolence. She was quick to joy, and her laughter seemed on the brink of transforming into something tangible.

Thin, gray-eyed, with golden brown hair, by the age of eighteen Constance had become a new symbol of Irish beauty. She and her sister Eva had spent their early years in the county Sligo, running through the woods of Lisadelle. W.B. Yeats, having fallen platonically in love with both of the Gore-Booth girls, rhapsodized them in his poetry.

The light of evening, Lissadell,
Great windows open to the south,
Two girls in silk kimonos, both
Beautiful, one a gazelle.

Having heard of Constance's beauty, Queen Victoria thought that such a girl would add some pleasant variety to Windsor.

The Gore-Booth spouses, wild from their daughter's immediate success in the society, hired a Frenchwoman to teach Constance how to curtsey without stepping on the train of her dress and walk on high heels without scratching the floor or injuring her ankles. Considering the impossible fashion of the eighties, no woman would survive without such lessons.

Nobody was particularly alarmed that in her childhood Constance, unlike most of her peers, preferred to dress up as a peasant girl instead of a princess or that she had developed a taste for rough potatoes. Her parents, uncommonly sympathetic landowners, who distributed free food to their tenants during the famine of 1880, did not interpret her behavior as a promise of a future rebellion. Not long after her grand debut in Windsor, the girl's heart stumbled over Aidan McCormack, a butler from Longford with nationalistic inclinations. Constance captured his thin face with slanted eyes and high cheekbones with a piece of charcoal on a sheet of thick ivory paper. To him she owed the birth of Isabel, her detachment from her circle of origin and her relentless devotion to the Celtic revival.

Constance's parents watched their pristine debutante suddenly turn into a suffragette. They had not expected that their demonstrations of compassion and generosity towards their tenants would lead their daughter into the arms of a penniless Gaelic butler. Feeding the hungry tenants did not in any way cancel out a future marriage to a man with a Saxon surname and preferably a title. Clearly, the overly imaginative girl had misinterpreted their lessons.

Blaming themselves for their eldest daughter's delusions, the Gore-Booth spouses did not have the heart to condemn her. The girl did not rebel, but simply took their teachings to the extreme. They could not demand for her to give up Aidan, and she could not demand for them to accept him. Humbly, they assumed the responsibility of raising Isabel, a rite they were destined to repeat years later with their second granddaughter Maeve.

Constance and Aidan had grown accustomed to the constant alternation of partings and reunions. Only the love that has neither goals nor conditions can withstand such trials. The addiction to freedom they shared bonded them tighter than any promises dictated by the tradition would. Constance felt no urgent need to weave a nest. Her matriarchal instincts had never developed fully. She saw Aidan whenever circumstances allowed, even after the two stopped being physically intimate. Even after marrying Count Markiewicz, another unbridled artist whom she met in Paris, Constance did not forget the handsome Fenian with whom she shared a child and a political vocation.

***

Aidan's arrest kept her sleepless. In Dublin she bribed everyone who came to mind, policemen and prison guards. Through her friend Molony, she received a vague story. Apparently, Aidan had been charged with an act of political treason committed during the Boer War more than ten years earlier. An anonymous witness recognized him to be the man who in 1899 convinced so many soldiers from Victoria's army to switch over to the Boers' side and assassinate their colonel.

Brendan could give her no advice on whether or not to believe the story. Aidan rarely shared his secrets, even with his most intimate friends. As for the Countess, she confessed that the theory struck her as a bit artificial.

"I suspect that it was a mere disguise, an excuse to arrest Aidan," she concluded. "They simply wanted to eliminate another influential Republican. He knows Michael Davitt in person and has connections in New York and Liverpool."

"But how the hell would the Brits know that?" Brendan asked. "'Tis not written 'pon his forehead, is it?"

"He had been betrayed, naturally. It's only a question by whom. One of his own men must have turned him in."

"Impossible!" Brendan objected. "Don't let your mind wander in that direction. Why, I've known these men for over twenty years and would put my hands in the fire for any one of them."

"You must be cautious about making such extravagant declarations," the Countess advised him with an air of menace. "You can hardly vouch for your own actions, let alone those of your comrades. What about the hapless boys in prison? They could have blurted out something against their own will. Do you have any idea what was done to them? There's that monstrous man by the name Felton. They've nicknamed him Master Inquisitor. Do you even know—"

"I know!" Brendan shouted so loudly that everyone shuddered and fell silent for a few seconds. "That I know," he continued in a lower voice, leaning closer to the Countess. "I saw what they did to my son. But if someone did betray Aidan, it wasn't Dylan. On that I would bet my very soul, if I still possess one. My boy is no traitor."

"I am dreadfully sorry about your personal tragedy," the Countess whispered, entwining her fingers around his arm, and fixed her eyes on the withering coals. "And I had hoped sincerely that the society had advanced since the times of Wolfe Tone. And to think that it was committed by those who claim themselves a superior breed! Such atrocities cannot go unpunished."

"And they won't," Brendan vowed. "The Brit I shot was just the first penny paid for our boys' blood. He seemed young, about Dylan's age. What will his father say? My lady... Constance... I hope you never learn the sorrow of outlivin' your own children. Such a trivial wish, you might say." Brendan paused and then squeezed his head, regretting his words. "Don't listen to me. Nothin' of this sort will happen to you. You're too fine a lady. God keep you and yours... I must've earned such sorrow. I must've angered the higher powers somehow. Didn't you know? I lost my younger one too, as if I'd never had him. All that I ever made my pride, he made his shame. At any rate, he's gone now, and he won't return in all likelihood. He's no better than dead."

Listening to Brendan, the Countess began toying with the idea of writing a manifesto on the subject of parental despotism and the disasters to which it can lead. She, herself, had resigned to a passive, observant kind of love when it came to her eldest daughter, rationing her maternal influence cautiously. With an aloof but still benevolent fascination she watched Isabel grow in the vast space provided for her.

"Ah, Brendan, you are a clever man," the Countess said at last, running her fingers up and down his arm, as if that superficial platonic caress could motivate him to change his mind. "Tell me now, what sort of world would it be, if all children, without exception, mirrored their parents?"

"I don't know. I've never given it much thought", Brendan replied in the tone of resignation. "And now I cannot think at all."

His brain abdicated. Perhaps the Countess' words held some truth worth considering, and the pressure of her fingers on his arm certainly gave him pleasure, but he knew that another thought would surely cause his skull to crack.

Now the presence of Fenians, the even murmur of their voices, the flickering of the bonfires produced a pacifying effect on him.

Without leaving the log on which he was sitting, Brendan dozed off.

Brendan awakened just as suddenly as he fell asleep, not knowing how much time passed since he had closed his eyes. He noticed, however, that someone's hands had tossed a few fresh bricks of wood into the fire and wrapped a heavy lambskin coat around his shoulders.

He glanced to his left and saw that the Countess was no longer there. Thaddeus McCluskey was sitting in her place, polishing the barrel of his rifle and whistling lowly.

"Our auburn-haired queen went back to Dublin," Thaddeus said. "She won't rest until she finds Aidan. I'm even tempted to say she loves him. What do you say, Malone?"

"I say she'll find his bones – if she's lucky."

"Bones are better than nothin' at all, I suppose. You can't say for sure 'tis over until you see the bones."

"Take your coat back, McCluskey. You didn't need to give it to me. I'm not that cold."

"Right enough!" Thaddeus winked all-knowingly. "Just look at your snout, bluer than a blueberry. I bet you haven't eaten anythin' either. Should you kick the bucket, none of us will benefit from it."

"Don't get your hopes up," Brendan growled. "I'm not dyin' just yet. Dyin' isn't that simple without an executioner's help. Tell me now: what do the rest of the lads mean to do?"

Thaddeus hummed pensively and rubbed his upper lip. He had not asked himself that question.

"I can't tell you," he said at last. "They're 'customed to Aidan orderin' them 'round. Now they're like a flock with no shepherd."

"We'll bring Aidan back," Brendan sprung up, cringing from the pain in his joints stiffened by the cold. "He won't sit in prison for much longer."

He climbed on the trunk of the fallen pine, making himself visible to everyone, and clapped his hands, "Quit chattin', gents! Come together, and we'll discuss a few matters."   A few small cliques silenced at once. The Fenians had been waiting for someone to finally stand up and speak up.

"Come closer now!" Brendan continued. "You can't hold back time by the tail. One way or another, Aidan got himself into trouble. Who knows what's bein' done to him now. They could've skinned him for the seventh time by now, and we're still sittin' here. I say, we go to Dublin."

Here Colin O'Nevin intervened.

"'Tis a dead cause, Bren. We know you mean well, but that just isn't possible. How can we free Aidan from a Dublin jail? The Countess herself failed, and she's got connections and money and devil knows what else. No, we won't save him. No chance of that. But we'll surely perish ourselves. Think how many heads will be severed all for nothin'."

Colin froze in the same pose with his arms spread widely, his head tilted on a side quizzically.

"O'Nevin's right," one of the men chimed in. "'Tis a dead cause."

The entire camp started grumbling. Brendan watched the Fenians, who only a minute ago looked to him with such eagerness, turn away, eyes lowered. Once again, anxiety and stupor overshadowed their faces.

"Well done, gents!" Brendan shouted, applauding mockingly. "Just like the Oath says. Why the deuce did we even take it? Oh, don't we all love singin' those patriotic ditties! Don't we all love gulpin' whiskey till it starts runnin' from our ears? But as soon as it comes down to business, forget the Oath, forget St. Lawrence

O'Toole! How quickly we start graspin' at our lives. One question: what the hell for?"

At his last words the grumbling subsided.

"Exactly how much are your lives worth now? Gents, let us be frank with ourselves. What great events do you foresee in your future? O'Nevin cannot be blamed, for he never gave the Oath. He's been pulled into this ordeal against his will. He's got three sons and two small daughters at home. He speaks for himself. But the rest of you who stare in the ground…yes, I'm referrin' to you, Leary, O'Grady, McLeod. Your sons are in prison. Those lads weren't even half your age, yet ten times braver. They had wives and children. And what do you have? What keeps you here? Your whistlin' and prancin'? Your pitchers of warm stout? Well, that didn't require takin' the Oath, now did it? If that's what you consider the core of Fenianism, then you're but a flock of sheep, bleatin' in vain. No wonder our British neighbors scoff at you."

"Come now," Colin attempted to reason with him. "A tad cheeky on your behalf, isn't it?"

"Not any harsher than any other piece of truth," Brendan parried, aware that his position was growing progressively precarious, yet still determined to go on. "Crucify me, if you wish, Brendan parried, aware that his position was growing progressively precarious, yet still determined to go on. There's no one here to stop you. Ungrateful buffoons! Aidan brought you together and led you for almost ten years. What would he think of you in his last hour? And why do you dread a trip to Dublin so? The Brits can't just gobble us up all at once, now can they?"

This time Colin could not answer. He only squeezed the elbow of his eldest son Liam, having seen the young man's jaw stiffened in determination.

"Liam, I'm warnin' you now," Colin whispered, "do nothin' foolish. Don't get yourself in another mess. Stay still, for your brothers' sake. For you know that if you dart fo'ward, they'll surely follow."

"Look now, I shan't beg you," Brendan concluded. "Stand and shake here like rabbits. If it comes to that, Thaddeus and I will go alone. Whatever becomes of us and Aidan, let it rest on your conscience, that's if you still got one. Here's my last call. Will anyone respond?"

"I shall!" cried Liam slipping from his father's grip. "I'll go, Mr. Malone. Count my brothers too. They're with me always. Matt, Doug! What're you waitin' for?"

The O'Nevin twins looked at each other, then at their older brother, who, eyes widened, ordered them to haste, and then almost simultaneously stepped forward.

A second later the three aged men, Leary, O'Grady and McLeod, joined the small regiment. They kept their heads down, still ashamed of their earlier faint-heartedness.

Brendan kept looking at the rest of the crowd. Under his glance more and more Fenians were coming forward, these men were determined to be heralded in history.

There was the old Basil Costello who was suffering from tuberculosis for the past year and could not think of a nobler fashion of ending his days than fighting for a comrade's freedom. There were Arthur Mallin and Will Cafferty, two veterans of the Second Boer War who had met Aidan on the sail to South Africa. They were joined by Tim Clancy, Maggie's former suitor whom she had rejected in Donnie's favor. Tim had never fully recovered from the blow. For months after the wedding he could be spotted wandering outside the cottage where Maggie lived with her new husband. Tim had not partaken in the revenge raid on the British garrison because he was out of town when the hell broke loose. He only learned about the rape and the skirmish after the executions had taken place. "Since 'tis too late to for me avenge the woman I once loved, the least I can do is help you free Aidan," he told his friends.

There were several youngsters, too: Seamus Donahue, Lucas Manohey, Eddie Callahan with his constant rival Dan Flannegan, and Brian McCullough. One by one they came forward and gathered around their new chieftain.

Solemnly, they carried their weapons: long-barreled hunting rifles, small hand guns and revolvers the possession of which was illegal, knives and daggers of all existing fashions and origins, sabers from every war of the past century. No two were of the same kind. What earthly powers could withstand a cause whose justice that had withstood time?

Brendan dreamed that he was standing on the border of the forest near his house, the same spot from which he shot the man in the British uniform. Only this time, instead of retrieving into the woods, he approached the corpse that was lying face down, grabbed it by the shoulder and flipped it over.

The same moment, he heard a low sigh and, not having the chance to see the dead man's face, turned. His eldest son was standing behind him.

Dylan looked more handsome than on his wedding day, his body whole and strong again. No bruises, no wounds were visible on his cheeks.

"Son…" Brendan whispered. "You're alive. You've returned."

Dylan's eyes became stern.

"No, Dadaí," his voice sounded remote, although he was standing only a few paces away. "I've come to fetch my brother."

"But Hugh's not here."

"Oh, he's here. Look!"

And he pointed at the dead man.

***

A sudden shove in the shoulder rescued Brendan from the nightmare. He opened his eyes and saw Liam O'Nevin's ivory face.

"What's wrong now?"

"'Tis our own Tim Clancy," Liam stammered. "I overheard him talkin' to Dan Flannegan. There's a small village nearby. An English family with a young daughter lives there. Tim kept urgin' Dan to go with him, but Dan refused. I didn't take my eyes off Tim all night, but then I dozed for a minute or so. When I came to, he was gone. We must hurry. He's plottin' his own revenge. He said he would…"

"Like bloody hell he will!" Brendan jumped up, grabbing his rifle. "God knows, we aren't wantin' for more trouble. Well, show me which way he went."

"Down the road, to the left," Liam explained hastily. "Mr. Malone, should I come along?"

"No, you stay here."

Thick hazelnut bushes closed behind Brendan's back. He found himself on a country road all traced with cartwheels. A narrow rye field lay at his right. Whoever endeavored to cultivate rye on that soil must have been an incurable optimist. Beyond that field, about a mile away, he saw a few burning dots, the windows of the houses.

Suddenly, a shadow crossed the moonlit path and disappeared in the rye. Brendan pursued that shadow down the corridor of the knocked down grain ears. Soon he heard heavy breathing in just a few yards ahead of him, and yelled, "Don't move!"

The rustle stopped, and only the sound of the panting remained. That sudden shout would paralyze anyone.

"Tim, I know 'tis you," Brendan continued. "I know what's on your mind. 'Tis a rotten thin', you know. In your place, I wouldn't do it."

"So, don't!" a malicious reply followed. "Keep away, Malone. I'll do to their whore what they did to Maggie. That wretched girl was done for when she married McCluskey rooster. A deadly mistake she'd made. You see, had she married me, none of this would've happened. I wouldn't have allowed it. Not for a day would I 'ev left 'er alone. Don failed to protect 'er. Off he went!"

"Leave Donnie McCluskey be," Brendan cut him off. "Donnie's dead."

"So bloody noble, are we! 'Twasn't one of your women that suffered. I'd like to see what would happen to your Christian piety."

"Still, 'tis a rotten thin'," Brendan continued. "We're Fenians, not some filthy brigands who go round villages by night, slayin' cattle and rapin' wenches. We only strike against Brits in uniforms. I'm warnin' you, Tim. Make one more step for'ard, and there will be no way back for you."

"What care I? So, don't take me back if you don't want to."

"That's not all," Brendan continued. "You'll never make your way of this field if you don't turn back this instant. I'm in command now. My men won't fall in the same pit as the enemy. I've got my rifle, Tim. Your relations would be sad to learn how you died. But if you come with me now, I won't say a word to anyone. Dan and Liam will also keep quiet, I promise. So, get your wits together and come with me."

What was it that made Tim turn around? Did his onslaught of malice subside or did he simply get frightened for his life? Whatever the reason was, he walked out of the rye onto the road.

In a gesture of reconciliation and almost paternal forgiveness, Brendan stretched his hand out, but Tim walked by.

"All is well," Brendan mumbled with a shrug. "Let the lad sulk. He'll recover."

After being convoyed to the camp, Tim leaned against an old oak, drew his knees up to his chest and thus spent the rest of the night, fully awake.

Liam O'Nevin and Dan Flannegan did not get any sleep either. They had spent the night smoking their pipes and whispering to each other. At dawn break they approached Tim and tried to spark a chat with him, trying to divert him from his suppressed rage.

"What's wrong with you, Timmy? Your eyes are like two steel nails," Dan made a clumsy joke.

Tim did not respond in any way. When the Fenians resumed their progress, he jumped back up on his horse, bearing the same facial expression. However, when they stopped in just a few miles from Dublin, Tim suddenly melted and volunteered his help with reconnaissance. The plan was to send a few men into the city to find out if the situation with Aidan had changed. The rest of the regiment was to remain in the forest.

"Mr. Malone," Tim began in a velvety voice. "I should be the one to go to Dublin. After all, I know the city better than anyone."

"Indeed, why shouldn't you, indeed?" Brendan responded, smiling to such unexpected enthusiasm. "Whom shall you take with you?"

"I need no one, honestly!" Tim patted his chest proudly. "I'll manage on my own. I've been to the city many a time. And I know how to talk to the British folk. If Aidan 'imself taught me how to carry on." He arched his brow all-knowingly. "One last thin', Mr. Malone. Thank you for stoppin' me last night. I wasn't thinkin' clearly. At times I horrify m'self. Maggie wouldn't have like that, I s'pose. I love 'er, you see. It maddened me that she chose Don, but it maddened me more than he couldn't save 'er. Now she's left a battered widow with three weanlin's. Ah, there's no use in fury! None of it can be undone. Can we shake hands now?"

"By God, we can," Brendan replied, offering his hand, like he did the night before. "I know you're a decent soul, Tim. But why do you wish to go by yourself? Perhaps, you should take Liam or Dan along?"

"Not to worry, Mr. Malone," Tim assured him, the calluses on their hand grinding against each other. "The police won't catch me. If there's a flood, I always come out dry. 'Tis in my nature."

I'll be sure to watch you dance on the gallows, old dog, Tim thought, sitting in the hall of police headquarters in Dublin. Pokin' rifles at me! Behold ye all, what a mighty chieftain we got here. So you defend the British wenches now? Well, the Brits will thank you heartily – with a rope 'round your neck. Before long, I'll have your lot out of my way. And the poor McCluskey widow shall become Mrs. Clancy. And the McCluskey brood shall call me Dadaí.

"Timothy Clancy?" a low-pitched voice called him.

Captain Lindell, a middle-aged Londoner, peered into the hall and beckoned Tim, whose knees began vibrating at the very first glance at that stiff, mustachios face. Still, there was a plan to carry through, so Tim assumed the most humble, most servile expression and entered the room.

There were a few more officers, only slightly younger than their captain but much livelier, judging from the howl their jokes raised. The bitter smell of cheap coffee and cigars saturated the air. It was lunchtime, and on top of the desk sat the leftovers of a shepherd's pie from the nearest culinary shop. The very sight of the filling spread all over the metal plate could kill appetite even in the flies circling above it. But apparently, the officers did not mind it and went on with their afternoon feast.

Then Lindell made them the sign to leave, and they obeyed, reluctant to leave the unfinished shepherd's pie.

"Winston!" he suddenly called on one of them. "If you run into Barkley later on today, tell him that Aidan McCormack's cell is already empty."

"So soon?" the young policeman asked.

"Not soon enough!" Lindell chuckled and stretched. "It has been empty since yesterday evening. The whole affair is over, rubbed into the ground. Relate that to Barkley, will you?"

Having dispatched his subordinates, the captain turned to face Tim, who all that time had been holding a groundhog's pose, rumpling his already shapeless cap.

"Mr. Clancy, please sit down," Lindell began, pointing at the leather-covered bench in the corner. "Speak. What urgent trouble did you wish to report?"

Tim inhaled profoundly, then clasped his hands and brought them to his lips. In that pose he spent a few seconds.

"I'm a peaceful man," he blurted out. "I've never harmed a soul or broken a law."

"I believe you gladly. You strike me as church choir material. Sadly, I have neither interest in your life story nor time to waste. What brings you here?"

"I've some news to impart from Roscommon." Tim spoke at a leisurely pace. He would not give in to the captain's pressure. The message he was about to deliver was certainly worth the wait. "I take it you don't know who I am or what I do."

"Are you the only Tim Clancy roaming Ireland?"

"I'm the only Tim Clancy who's been servin' Mr. Howard and Mr. Felton in Roscommon. They told me you'd recognize their names."

Lindell knitted his graying eyebrows. "Exactly what sort of work have you been doing for them?"

"Shall we say...I've keepin' them informed of...developments in the community. I've been helpin' them maintain peace and order by pointin' out the troublemakers. As you well know, after Clarke's return from America, there's been some stirrin' within the IRB. They've been followin' Aidan McCormack, that sleepless lunatic who'd fought in the last Boer War. He took all he'd learned in the British army and imparted it onto his men. He was groomin' 'em for another insurrection."

"You can stop worrying about McCormack," the captain said, slamming a folio with Aidan's name against the tabletop. "He's gone."

"But his men are still lookin' for him," Tim continued. "They're on the loose, preparin' to strike. Their sons staged a skirmish 'gainst the British soldiers who got a bit carried away with the wrong woman. Surely, you've heard of that. They took some landowner's wife for a whore, and the village goons went frantic over it. *Fenian pride, Fenian revenge*! You could hear their cries across the river. *Fenian this, Fenian that...* You know how their breed loves their martyrs. They've tasted of British blood and now they hunger for more. It won't be long before they shoot more servants of the crown. There's one man in particular who presents more dangerous than the rest. Brendan Malone is his name. He's the father of Dylan Malone, one of the executed. Now that McCormack is gone, they chose Malone the new centre. He's taken over the circle. He simply stood there, wavin' his rifle, and they flocked to him. I tell you, Captain, he's got men behind him, and they've got weapons."

"Well, Mr. Clancy, do you know where they are at this moment?"

"I know where I left 'em. I've got a handful of them waitin' in the woods."

"What does a 'handful' mean to you, Mr. Clancy?" Tim's signature Celtic imprecision was irritating the captain. "If I am to issue orders, I need to know how many men I should bring with me."

"There's 'bout thirty of them, forty at most," Tim replied without hesitation. "I doubt they got reinforcements. They're secluded in the forest, and they don't know the land very well. It shan't be hard for you to round them up."

Having made a sign for Tim to remain seated, Captain Lindell walked out into the hallway and summoned his junior officers. The high ceilings in the police building distorted their voices.

Tim did not strain his ears to catch what they were saying to each other. Not that it was any of his concern at this point. He had fulfilled his duty as informer. The rest was up to the authorities.

Fifteen minutes later the captain returned. "Mr. Clancy, you are free to go. My men and I shall take over this matter."

Tim was not ready to leave just yet. "When exactly do I get comp'sated for my services?" he asked bluntly.

"Take it up with Howard and Felton," Lindell replied with a shrug. "It is with them that you forged your deal. Don't give me that look, Mr. Clancy. I'm not authorized to pay anyone, not even my own men. It's taxing enough to issue orders. Go back to Roscommon. I'm certain that Howard will pay you, once our mission is accomplished."

Dealing with the likes of Tim Clancy was one of the most unpleasant parts of Lindell's job, even though he realized informers were a necessary evil. Even after twenty years of service, he still found himself disgusted by certain elements of his job.

"I don't have a penny for the train ride home."

The captain inflated his cheeks, slapped himself on the pocket, drew out three shillings and tossed them on the floor in front of Tim.

"This is all I have. Take it. Go."

Towards midnight, the chatters in the camp turned into scarce whispers and finally abated. Still, very few Fenians considered sleep, disquieted by Tim Clancy's prolonged absence still had not returned. They sat in packs, shoulder to shoulder, or alone, leaning against a tree.

Old Basil Costello struggled to his feet and declared that he wanted to look for fresh water, because his body refused to thrive on whiskey alone. Nobody stopped him. Aware of his rapidly progressing illness and his necessity to feel useful, the Fenians allied to protect his waning sense of self-worth by giving him tasks he still could perform. Just in case he would find a spring, they handed him a dozen empty flasks.

"Be careful," Brendan advised him.

"Don't ye fret, Basil won't yield easily," the old man replied and dissolved in the shrubbery.

Forty minutes elapsed. Nobody even thought of reviving the withering campfires.

Liam O'Nevin pulled the cross from beneath his shirt and held it to his lips, then placed his hands on the heads of his younger brothers sitting at his either side, and started praying quietly. Infected by the universal solemnity, the boys drew closer to him.

Observing the three, Brendan involuntarily thought of his deceased brother Declan, the peacemaker and the wise man of the family. Declan Malone seemed to possess an innate knowledge of truths and mysteries that others fail attain over a lifetime. It was him Brendan addressed when God seemed too remote.

"Speak to the Almighty for me and my mates. He'll listen to you. It won't be long until I face Him myself. I feel death all too close. It stands some ten yards away, rustlin' in the bushes, breathin' chilly wind in my face. Tell Him, I'm sorry for what I did wrong, knowingly or not. Tell Him, Brendan Malone is willin' to pay the price."

***

The sudden crackling of branches made the Fenians spring up. They saw Basil Costello's horse and heard the dull jingle of the water flasks against the empty saddle.

"Basil!" cried Thaddeus McCluskey. "Where the hell is he?"

"Anythin' could've happened," Leary replied. "How could you let him go? That's it! I'm off to find him right now."

"Don't move!" O'Grady ordered. "Or we'll have to look for you. If that goes on, we'll all be wanderin' like lost sheep."

Brendan interrupted them.

"Hush up you all! I hear somethin'. Sounds like horsemen, 'bout half a mile away, comin' from the east."

"I hear them from the west, too," Liam added. "Christ! Are they bringin' a whole cavalry here?"

The noises grew louder. The horsemen were coming from both sides. By the way the sound of the hooves spread through the forest, one could guess they formed a circle.

Brendan wavered, his pallor noticeable even in the dark. Colin O'Nevin grabbed him by the shoulders with both hands.

"It's a trap! Wake up, Malone, you bloody idiot! Clancy sold us out. He brought the soldiers here. They killed Basil, and now they'll rip our heads off. We're dead men now, all b'cause of you!"

"Not dead yet," Brendan answered, regaining his senses and shoving Colin aside. "We've got horses and weapons, too. We'll break through!"

As soon as he finished that phrase, the bushes parted, and the first soldiers rode into the camp.

Two seconds later Arthur Mallin gasped and grabbed his throat, blood spraying through his fingers. He looked at his slippery hands with bewilderment and fell right under the horse of the Englishman who shot him.

This first death awakened the Fenians who had frozen up at the sight of the adversary. Instantly, they became blind to the uniforms of the British, their rifles and their numbers. Still, the resulting slaughter was nothing unique, nothing to which the Irish had not grown accustomed over the past seven centuries. No resolution is more trivial, more formulaic than a pack of Celts gracing the tips of Saxon bayonets. It happened under Robert Emmet in 1803, Daniel O'Connell in 1848 and James Stephens in 1867. It was bound to happen again in 1916 under Patrick Pearse, the maddest and the most unforgettable one. It appeared as if one rebellious spirit traveled through time, possessing one body after another, hitting head after head against the same wall.

The Fenians dropped before even reaching their horses. For every wounded British soldier there were three dead Irishmen.

Sixteen-year old Matt O'Nevin tripped over his twin brother's corpse. The boy stopped in the middle of the turmoil, no longer hearing the screams and the shooting. He knelt near Douglas; it was not his fate to stand up again. A bullet hit him in the temple, and he dropped his bleeding head on his brother's chest. The two were born on the same day and died almost simultaneously.

Eddie Callahan, a brawler each ordinary day, unbridled his temper in the battle. Having spotted the soldier that killed Daniel Flannegan, Eddie cleaved the glossy neck of the Englishman's horse with his saber. The gorgeous beast pranced, and the soldier, startled by the young Irishman's nerve, lost his balance. A second later his own neck was split with the very same saber.

Eddie made a mistake by taking too long a time to admire his handiwork in a place that permitted not a second of forgetfulness. A lance went into his lung from the back. Eddie jerked forward, spitting the blood on the grass, turned around, facing the one who attacked him and immediately received another wound between his ribs. Still, he grabbed the lance and held on to it until the only remaining color before his eyes was black.

Will Cafferty was lying with his face down into the autumn leaves, his arms spread apart, as if trying to embrace the ground, still shuddering each time a horse's hoof stepped on his back.

Tom McCullough looked as if he were taking a leisurely rest against the tree. But the red stain on the breast pocket of his shirt was growing wider, and his head hung at an unnatural angle.

Brian, Tom's nephew, was nowhere to be seen, neither among the fighters nor among the corpses. Lucas Mahoney and Denis Leary also disappeared. Brendan assumed that God simply helped them escape.

Because those few Fenians managed to break through the circle, the battle became somewhat less congested, and the adversaries dissipated through the woods.

Well done, lads! Brendan rejoiced silently.

Then his eyes paused at Liam O'Nevin. The boy was panting, dragging his leg behind and covering a lance wound in his shoulder with his hand. After seeing his brothers fall dead, he was running at random with a savage face.

Brendan jumped off his horse.

"Get on, and get out!"

Liam stopped, stupefied.

"Quick! Get out while you can!"

The boy still lingered. Brendan forced him into the saddle and fired right by the horse's ear. The animal shuddered and took off, carrying Liam away and leaving its former master behind.

When Brendan looked around, he realized that he was completely alone among the remaining soldiers. Having no other target in their sight, they rushed at him all at once, although he made no attempt to escape. For some time Captain Lindell studied the Fenian in the same manner as Pontius Pilate studied Christ, with more fascination than fury. He would have stared at him even longer, had his men not returned.

"They escaped. We lost sight of them."

That remark awakened the captain, but only partially.

"They couldn't have gotten too far," he said. "Tomorrow we'll send more troops and do a thorough search."

"How much you still got to learn 'bout us," Brendan suddenly spoke out. "After seven centuries in this land you still don't know a darn 'bout its people. Go on and send your men out by hundreds to catch a handful of us."

He narrowed his eyes, savoring some thought; five lads were flying north through the woods, half-conscious, pressing to their horses' necks. Ulster is no small province, with plenty asylums. Ten, fifteen years later Liam O'Nevin would enter a nameless pub in Antrim, Armagh, or Fermanagh and raise a glass of whiskey to the men he had once known.

"Now, wasn't that a merry spectacle?" Brendan continued. "Merrier than you expected, I bet. Well, there'll more surprises for you to come. And I'll be sure to watch it. Oh, I won't blink my eye."

They tied him to the trunk of an oak. At first Brendan was perplexed, but then he understood that they wanted a ceremony. They have done enough raw killing, and now it was time for a solemn, methodical execution. In a strange way it gladdened Brendan, because he desired a painful death. Now he was eager to receive all the fires in the world, all the smoke and the steel, to share the sufferings of his comrades and especially his son, the fleshy sufferings that he eluded most of the time. But what could possibly get through to a frenzied Fenian who had lost his fear?

"Forgive me, Lord, for I've not loved my enemy."

Those were the last words of the rebel.

His body mingled with the wood of the tree. The old oak received his heart, and the roots absorbed his blood.

When the corrosive fog over his eyes dissipated, he began perceiving human figures and hearing voices, not of the enemies surrounding the tree, but of his friends with whom he parted just a few minutes ago. Two figures struck him as particularly familiar. Two young men stepped forward. In the autumn sunlight leaking through the half-bare branches, their faces glimmered like golden wax.

"*Dia duit, Dadaí,*" the eldest one greeted him in flawless Gaelic.

"You're with us now," the youngest one added in English.

(Belfast, Davis Street, Denis McCullough's house)

Early autumn in Northern Ireland was a time of exquisite reserved beauty, of street festivals, bagpipe marches, harp concerts and organ recitals at St. Anne's. Sunlight streamed over the Cathedral Quarter like diluted honey. Bulmer Hobson was beginning to feel the effects of the season, his Dublin romance with Helena Molony being in a state of indefinite recession once again. He drowned his nostalgia in black tea with nutmeg. Perhaps, he longed for something stronger, but his Quaker belief in the benefit of sobriety held him back. Besides, he feared that if he added whiskey to his tea, his memory would transport him back into Helena's flat on Abbey Street. He would feel her clingy hot fingers on his shoulders and her glossed mouth on his neck, and that memory alone would suffice to render him useless to his country. Love and alcohol had a debilitating effect on him, and he simply could not allow that. In order to serve Ireland, he had to remain sober and abstinent. Once again, this tall, athletic twenty-seven-year old had to embrace the inner monk. The oversized tweed coat, the unofficial uniform of Sinn Fein and IRB members, became his cassock, his shield from the world of sensual temptations.

Since lack of employment prevented Bulmer from living in the capitol, he did everything in his power to keep the nationalist movement ablaze in his native Belfast. His main effort was to revive the Dungannon Clubs movement, one of his earliest enterprises that he started with Denis McCullough five years earlier. In their own words, the purpose of the clubs was "to build up Ireland and regain political independence". Equipped with propaganda leaflets and slides, the young men roamed the North, delivering anti-unionist speeches and attracting like-minded enthusiasts. Those expeditions involved a certain risk of being stoned by the mob. The North was in no hurry to convert to nationalism. Denis had a scar on his forehead as a reminder of one of his early sermons on a street corner in Belfast.

One breezy September evening, as the members of the Dungannon Club were preparing for another public meeting, Denis McCullough brought a copy of *The Belfast Telegraph* from the street.

"You may want to read this, Hobson," he told his colleague, waving the newspaper like he would a surrender flag. "Or, I should rather say, this is *not* something you want to read."

"What's this, McCullough?" The question was purely mechanical. Bulmer was busy arranging the slides he had prepared for his lecture on immigration.

"There was a skirmish in Roscommon."

"Allow me to guess: an evicted tenant hit a landlord on the head with a shovel?" Bulmer had trouble imagining that anything newsworthy could possibly happen in the province of Connaught. "I am expected to lose sleep over this?"

"You may have to for a few nights, Hobson. You know I wouldn't trouble you over a trifle. This story you must read, as it involves the IRB."

Bulmer set the slides aside and snatched the newspaper from his colleague's hands. After ten seconds of reading, a seizure of fury ran across his clean boyish face. "What the bloody hell is this! Some aging idiot from Tulsk staged an insurrection? An entire IRB circle is wiped out!"

"Easy, Hobson!" Denis attempted to pacify his frazzled colleague. "We do not know what truly happened. We only know how the British journalists say about it. What do you expect from a vehemently unionist paper? You want them to paint a flattering picture of the IRB? Naturally, they stretched the truth as far as they could. They will do anything to portray one of us in the ugliest light imaginable."

Bulmer crumpled the newspaper and threw it on the table in disgust. "There is a limit to how far the truth can be stretched, McCullough! All I know is that IRB members were involved in armed hostilities, without the approval of the Supreme Council. Just look at the title of the article: *Fanatical Fenian Initiates Vengeance Massacre*. Now every other Fenian shall endeavor the same, just to find his name in the headlines! What will be left of the IRB? You and I labor day and night just to find the right men and instruct them in the ways of the Brotherhood. Then some senile peasant from Tulsk uses *our* men for his personal revenge schemes."

Denis was beginning to regret showing the article to his colleague. Truth be told, he did not expect such a violent reaction out of Bulmer, who was not generally prone to dynamite explosions and expressed his indignation in a calm, methodical manner. "Come, Hobson, show some leniency towards Malone. The man was driven by fury, which is entirely plausible."

"Plausible, perhaps, but still inexcusable! Malone acted on an impulse, which is a luxury no Fenian is allotted. His behavior goes against the Oath, which explicitly dictates that no hostilities are to be initiated without the approval of one's superior officers. Malone and his eldest son just grabbed their hunting rifles and went after the Brits. Welcome back to 1867!"

"Listen to yourself, Hobson!" Denis reproached him. "An Irishwoman was brutally violated in her own home by a flock of drunken Brit soldiers, and you preoccupy yourself with oaths and rules. It must be a hangover from your Quaker days. Written rules above your innate sense of justice! Have you no heart?"

"Believe it or not, McCullough, I do have a heart—to my great inconvenience," Bulmer replied in his sonorous staccato voice. "I am just as enraged as anyone else, for I, too, have a sister and a mother. Still, I do not allow my heart to dictate my actions. My impulses do not overrule the Fenian constitution. We are not a squad of amateur avengers, nor are we chastity police. We cannot rise up in arms every time a tenant gets evicted or a woman gets raped." Bulmer began pacing around the hall, flexing his fists and hyperventilating. "How are we to free this country if we waste all our strength on vain bloodshed? There is no order in our ranks, no sense of hierarchy, no discipline, no plan... There's only reckless rage... And we all know how far it had led us in the past. There will always be causes for rage. Don't you see, McCullough? We must get rid of the unruly old drunks in the IRB and replace them with a new sober generation that can exercise self-restraint. Malone took criminal liberties, and I shall see that no Fenian regards him as a hero. Are you listening? Malone will be remembered as a frivolous and insubordinate upstart, someone who had compromised the entire IRB."

Denis had great many things to say to his opinionated colleague, but chose not to vocalize them. He could have said, "Hobson, you haven't risen up the IRB ranks yourself. It is not your place to judge a fallen brother, even if he had violated the rules." After six years of working side by side with Bulmer, Denis knew that there was no use in arguing with him, at least not while he was in a state of righteous indignation. Bulmer had his own vision of absolute truth and was prepared to defend it. He had openly shared with Denis his designs to one day take over the IRB. Given Bulmer's supernatural energy and self-confidence, it was not such a far-fetched possibility. That was the risk Denis took when he introduced the young Quaker to the brotherhood back in 1904.

"Do try to collect yourself, Hobson," Denis said at last and took his seething friend by the shoulders. "We have a meeting to attend."

***

(Surrey House, Leinster Road, Rathmines, Dublin – Countess Markiewicz's residence)

In late October, the women of *Inghinidhe na hÉireann*, the Daughters of Ireland, were welcoming a new member. Even though the organization had been in existence since 1900, the novelty of the initiation ceremony had not worn off for the founder Maud Gonne, who had been a matriarchal figure for all free-spirited young women in Ireland regardless of their religion or social standing. There was only one requirement for joining, and a very simple one: whole-hearted commitment to fight for Ireland's full independence from England. Disenchanted supporters of the British crown often make the most fervent Irish nationalists. Being in their ranks herself, Maud Gonne understood that better than anyone. Like her friend Countess Markiewicz, she had detached from her English roots in favor of Ireland. For that very reason, Maud had exerted every effort to make the initiation especially solemn for this particular newcomer.

There were over thirty ladies gathered in the reception room on that night, with Countess Markiewicz and Helena Molony presiding over them. They all both rose to their feet when Maud, following a trail of candles illuminating the hall, ushered their new sister, a pale blonde Englishwoman in her mid-twenties, with strong pliant fingers. The bottom hook of her meticulously tailored black jacket was undone: the young woman was about four months into her pregnancy.

"Ladies, it is my privilege to introduce to you Mrs. Edith Malone, a gifted linguist and musician from Belfast. She received her musical training in London, and she is already fluent in French and Italian. Now she is looking forward to learning Gaelic. Let us welcome Mrs. Malone into our midst."

Countess Markiewicz presented her with a broche and Molony with a green and gold sash. After the first volley of applause had subsided, the newcomer stepped forward to deliver her first speech.

"I do not know how many of you are familiar with my story," she began in a low even voice, as there were no more sobs left in her throat. "Hugh, my late husband, was not a Fenian or even a fervent patriot. Still, he was an Irishman, whose heart ached for his country. After the executions in Roscommon, he was found dead outside his own house, presumably shot by one of his compatriots, possibly even by a family member. After becoming widowed, I found myself unable to rejoin the community in my native Belfast. The people who had been my steady clients for years had all unanimously agreed that they did not want their children to take music lessons from someone related to the Malones of Tulsk. As a sister-in-law of a convicted criminal, I was an unwholesome influence. Hugh was right after all. It only takes a drop of poison to ruin a glass of wine. But I am not here because I need shelter. I come to you not out in desperation, but in determination. Time has come for me to stop pretending that I can live in this country and claim or feign neutrality. My husband insisted on remaining apolitical, and he was killed nonetheless. If I am to continue living in Ireland, I must choose a side. It's either the English crown or the Irish republic. Having examined my conscience, I choose the latter. It is most ironic that I should feel compelled to fight the very war from which my own late husband had abstained, but I cannot blind my eyes to the transgressions of the race from which I sprung. And now, at the age of twenty-five, I look forward to my rebirth, as I commit myself to your cause."

Mrs. Malone's mixture of poise and unsentimental bluntness brought on another volley of cheer. The stoic young Englishwoman, recently rejected by Belfast, found herself locked inside a ring of fluttering hands and velvet hats with wavering feathers. Her eyes perfectly dry and wide-open, Edith surveyed her new family.

In the middle of the jubilation, Countess Markiewicz leaned over to Helena Molony and whispered' "It grieves me that my own daughter is not here to witness the initiation. She was fond of Hugh. I believe she would take particular delight in meeting his wife – now his widow."

"Poor darling Isabel," the young actress replied. The two women, who had attended countless meetings and ceremonies together, were accustomed to whispering to each other over the noise. They did not need to raise voices. "Who would've thought that her father's death would have such a devastating effect on her? Truth be told, I never received the impression that the two were particularly close. In conversation with me she had made some rather unflattering comments regarding his leadership."

"I don't believe that Aidan's death is the main culprit of her melancholy. Isabel blames herself for the destruction of the entire IRB circle. All those boys she had lured into the Brotherhood. I bet it was Bulmer Hobson who sowed that guilt in her heart. Wouldn't I like to strangle that mouthy Quaker! He sent Isabel a letter after which she could not stop crying for days. My maternal instinct, however stunted, is telling me just that. Really, I ought to know better what is happening in my own daughter's heart."

"Perhaps, I should talk to Isabel," Helena proposed. "I hope she comes to the next editorial meeting of *Bean na hÉireann*. Do you by chance know where she is right now?"

"To be perfectly honest, I don't have a faintest idea," the Countess confessed. "What a monstrous thing for a mother to say!"

The two women stopped applauding and glanced at each other.

"My dear Constance, there are more monstrous things coming," Helena said, her eyes exuding some prophetic exultation. "Raise your sails and prepare for a tempest. All the tiny voices in my head keep telling me that we shall have one hellish decade."

About the Author

Marina Julia Neary is an award-winning historical essayist, multilingual arts & entertainment journalist, novelist, dramatist and poet. Her areas of expertise include British steam-punk, French Romanticism and Irish nationalism. Her novel *Wynfield's Kingdom* (Fireship Press, 2009) was featured in the March 2010 edition of First Edition Magazine in the UK, followed by the sequel *Wynfield's War* in 2010. She is the author of two historical plays, *Hugo in London* (licensing available through Heuer), and the sequel *Lady with a Lamp: the Untold Story of Florence Nightingale* (illustrated edition available through Fireship Press). Her poems have been organized in a collection *Bipolar Express* (Flutter Press, 2010). Her sci-fi novelette *My Salieri Complex* is available as an e-book through Gypsy Shadow Press. *Brendan Malone: the Last Fenian* is her first novel exploring early 20th century Irish nationalism. Neary currently serves as an editorial reviewer and steady contributor for Bewildering Stories magazine.

ALL THINGS THAT MATTER PRESS ™

FOR MORE INFORMATION ON TITLES AVAILABLE FROM
ALL THINGS THAT MATTER PRESS, GO TO
http://allthingsthatmatterpress.com
or contact us at
allthingsthatmatterpress@gmail.com

www.ingramcontent.com/pod-product-compliance
Lightning Source LLC
Chambersburg PA
CBHW031110260626
47172CB00001B/302